April, Maybe June

Shalanna Collins

A Bliss Sisters Magical Adventure

April, Maybe June

Shalanna Collins

Los Angeles Santa Barbara

APRIL, MAYBE JUNE

A Muse Harbor Publishing Book

PUBLISHING HISTORY

Muse Harbor Publishing paperback edition
published March 2014

Published by Muse Harbor Publishing, LLC

Los Angeles, California

Santa Barbara, California

Cover artwork by Ted Hayward

www.tedhayward.com

ISBN 978-1-61264-146-1

Visit Muse Harbor Publishing at

www.museharbor.com

To all you Aprils,
whoever you are.

acknowledgements

I'd like to acknowledge the long mentorship and friendship of the denizens of the Fido WRITING echo and its ensuing mailing list, especially author Dennis M. Havens, who has suffered through draft after draft of my various books. Thank you, all of my beta readers over the years. Most of all, I am thankful for the fantastic editing input and support received from my editor, Dave Workman. I've been blessed in many ways so that I could make this book a reality. I appreciate the support of my husband, mother, late mother-in-law, and most of my family members. Especially Teddy!

april and june

My sister June and I are lounging in the tree-house when I spy the black-and-white police car.

"June, look." She ignores me as I point, my finger following the copmobile as it prowls the gentle curve down Buttonwood Lane. She is busy checking out dishy Justin Fink, ninth grade sex god, as he suns himself next door beside his family's pool like a spoiled cat. "Is it slowing down?"

June finally swivels the telescope and points it out front. It's not a pro model, more of a toy for close-up viewing of (for example) the freckles around Justin's belly button. Even without it, from up here we can see all the way from our hilltop to the "Welcome to Renner, Texas—home of the Mighty Ocelots" billboard at the entrance to our ritzy subdivision. The crow's-nest view from the century oak in the far back corner of our wooded slope is the main reason we still use this back-yard kiddie perch, although I just turned thirteen and June is a large fourteen-and-a-half.

"Two officers, looks like." She twists the focus ring. "Stopping right in front of our house."

"Oh, my God." I fall back against the tree trunk, shaking the ancient branches ever so slightly.

June punches my upper arm, where she keeps a perma-bruise going for easy control. "Get a grip, Cruelest." My name is April, but she thinks it's funny to call me that, out of some famous poem or another that Gary (our parents, Gary and Lynwood, are progressive and believe that first-name basis relationships within the family provide for a level playing field and improved self-esteem) loves to quote. "They're probably going to the neighbors across the street." She closes her eyes as if indulging a hopeless idiot yet again.

"June. LOOK." I shake her by the shoulders.

Finally my sister opens her eyes. She won't yield the eyepiece, but peers through the scope again. "They're getting out. Heading up the front walk. About to ring our bell." Despite the gravity of the situation, she snickers at the sexual allusion.

My heart skips a beat. "What could they want? Has Lynwood got that many unpaid tickets? No, it's Gary. Could he get arrested like Uncle Ray?"

"Shut up, Cruelest. You're hysterical." But she looks a bit perturbed.

"It's something bad." Surely it isn't about the many MP3s and torrents that June downloads daily from pirate sites. "Didn't he pay enough taxes?" My heart feels squeezed.

"That would be the IRS, and besides, you're obsessed because Ray 'forgot' to pay any for ten years." According to Lynwood, our cousin Arlene became a Fallen Woman because of her father's ruin. "Gary has Lynwood sign the forms every year. I always hear her whining about how confusing they are to read, but he insists she mustn't sign anything she hasn't read. So he's filing." Her forehead wrinkles, which is a sure sign that she's taking this seriously. "Now be quiet so I can think."

"Ever since he started working from home, I've been worried." I stick my index finger in my mouth and gnaw the cuticle. It's a habit I'm trying to break.

"Please." My sister reaches for my perma-bruise, but I scoot out of reach. "He's an independent contractor and he knows what he's doing. He wouldn't risk it all for some stupid deal. More like maybe there's been an accident, or somebody died."

This does not calm me.

Her eyes look worried, for once. "We're going in."

Our house is a forties mansion that Lynwood extensively remodeled with Gary's long-suffering help, with a yard that's three-quarters of an acre, like the others around it. It's a traditional Texas ranch, but two wings were added on at angles over the years, so the room layout is fairly offbeat. That's why, for instance, the master bedroom sticks out into the back yard and is the closest entry point from the treehouse.

We sneak inside through Lynwood's antique French doors and sidle up the bedroom hallway to the coat closet, where we can hear what's going on in the front room. It's freaky: June is a ninja who can do the stealth trick—she can creep up behind you like a wraith and startle your teeth out, which I don't understand because she's downright chunky where I'm slender—whereas I always knock something over and a klieg spot clicks on overhead.

So of course my shin bangs against the doorframe as I dodge to try to see around June. Twisting away, I trip and fall sprawling into the room in full view, my voice yelping without my permission, and I am caught.

The police turn their heads. There's an African-American woman who's what I would call statuesque and a short, balding white man who looks mean. They don't jump up off the loveseat to assume battle positions pointing guns or anything, but I can tell my "discovery" has put them on a higher level of alert.

But Gary only says, "We're busy, April. Go study."

"Just a moment," says the female cop. "Is this your daughter, ma'am?"

Don't you hate it when people look straight at you and then talk about you to someone else as if you're some kind of pet? Scrambling to my feet, I brush myself off to show I'm unhurt. I paste on the uncertain-kid grin and blink a few times for effect.

"Yes, my daughter, April Bliss," Lynwood says with a weak smile. She flutters her fingers. "Go on, now, hon."

The male cop looks at me squinty-eyed. I know why: it's because I don't look like I could belong to her. Lynwood is so gorgeous, like some movie star. He finally asks Lynwood, "Other children in the house?"

"My older sister, June." Why shouldn't I be allowed to talk? I'm as good as anybody here.

The female officer looks as if she might laugh, but bites it back. Good. People can make fun of our names being months and all, but it beats "Frances Marion," which is what Lynwood's was until she changed it. Lynwood Bliss. Sounds like a fairy princess.

"She idolizes her big sister," says Lynwood in the moony voice of a simp. "I'm so glad my girls get along."

I definitely do *not* idolize June. What I do is try to keep an eye on her and watch out for her. Because really, she's very vulnerable.

"Why aren't you in school?" the male officer asks me. Nobody asks this about Justin Fink lazing away the afternoon by the pool—he's on work-study and gets out at noon. Of course I look ten years old, skinny and short with a baby face, so they ask.

"We're homeschooled," I reply, bracing for the knowing nods. At least Lynwood's not like one of those stage
mothers who always tell people how precocious their
Special Snowflakes are and what an advanced vocabulary they have. Even though I am and I do—but no one
knows, as I usually don't get more than a few words in
edgewise for some reason.

"All right," is all the woman officer says. Lynwood
makes the sign for "go away" in American Sign Language (which looks like she's yanking her right eyebrow
off with her right hand). She started teaching us last year
so we'd all have a Secret Communication Skill in quiet
places like museums and such, but June firmly pretended
not to understand a finger-crook of it until Lynwood
lost interest. Gary winks and waves me upstairs.

I guess I'm dismissed.

I skulk up to my room, acting properly chastened for
wanting to know what's going on in my own family.

June has secreted herself somewhere and is probably
still eavesdropping. I expect to find her listening from
the top of the stairs, but no. She's not in the hall and not
in her room. Like I said, a ninja. She never gets caught.

In a few minutes she plops down on my bottom bunk
and punches the intercom's LISTEN button. (Gary and
Lynwood never remember that it's been fixed and is
working again. Maybe June fixed it herself without telling them.)

Voices boom through the silver speaker, tinny but un-
derstandable.

"I'm sure it's simply a family misunderstanding." Lynwood sounds squeaky. "Arlene's probably with one of her friends, staying at somebody's house, trying to scare her parents."

"Doesn't look that simple, Mrs. Bliss," says the male officer.

"Arlene knows better than to take drugs, let alone sell them to children," Lynwood says insistently.

Gary's voice holds that dangerous note as he orders her, "Just answer the detective's questions, dear."

"We've checked this out pretty thoroughly, ma'am, and it looks serious. If you hear from Arlene Bruce, will you call this number?"

"We'll be sure to let you know if we come across any information." Gary sounds distant, as if he's already mentally escorting them out. "But I'm sure this will all work itself out. Things like this usually do."

June's evaluation: "Bullshit. Something's going on."

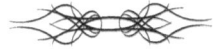

At last the cops leave. Our parents are arguing louder in their bedroom now that they think we're asleep, Lynwood having quietly checked on us. June suggested we play possum and I went along with it, although I'm hungry. Dinnertime came and went and nobody acknowledged it but my growling tummy.

Gary's after Lynwood about how much she told the cops. "I wish you'd let me call that Perry Mason type from your office. What's his name? The guy with the beard. We should never have talked to them without a lawyer present, not once we found out they want to take Arlene in." Gary sounds like he does when one of us screws up pretty badly. "If I'm gonna be questioned by the police, I'm gonna have a lawyer. Doesn't matter, I just flat don't trust cops. Not that they aren't doing a good job—overall, they are—and not that they aren't performing a much needed service. Still, mistakes are made and I don't want to be one of them." He always starts blathering when he doesn't know what to do.

"I don't care what you do, but I'm going to call my sister."

"Worst mistake you could make." Gary sounds firm. "If Odile wanted us to know, trust me, she'd have called you. Keep out of this, or they'll think you're involved. The police are already suspicious because you were too eager to cooperate."

"I'm worried about Arlene. I wanted to help."

"Never volunteer stuff they don't ask," Gary practically shouts.

Apparently, before we could get inside to overhear, Lynwood spilled her guts to the police. Fortunately there wasn't much to spill. Lynwood starves herself to stay fashionably thin.

Lynwood is sobbing now and Gary is comforting her, apologizing for going off on her like that. That scene always ends in a make-out session, so I reach over to click the intercom off. I'm not *that* liberal-minded.

June muses aloud. "I wonder, why does it always sound like the citizen is the bad guy when the cops show up? If you say you want them to get a warrant instead of letting them come right in and toss your house, or demand a lawyer be present at an interrogation, they look at you as if you are a hardened criminal. Does that make sense?"

"Not to me. But then I'm merely a starving student." My stomach roars really loud. "Aren't you hungry?"

"Ravenous. Come on." She sits up, tossing her longish hair back over her shoulder, and we head to her room. June pulls out some of her contraband, but most of it is sugary and salty, junk snacks that I don't prefer.

Lynwood forgets that other mammals require actual sustenance. But she and Gary are upset and too busy to think about us, so this is the best I'm going to get. I take a couple of sacks of chips back to my room and bed down with a new fantasy novel I've been saving for a special occasion. Witches and dragons will take my mind into other realms for distraction.

I'm sure this will all blow over soon.

along comes trouble

At four A. M. something startles me awake.

I don't just come awake a little groggy, but pop to full alertness. My breaths sound deafeningly loud. I lie there still as a stone, listening.

Because I'm sure there was a noise.

I hear it again: a series of quiet pings off my window glass.

I'm not dumb enough to blindly peek out the window. I have to be sure they can't see in, though I can see out. There's a full moon (Gary says that's when all the crazies come out, and everyone who was about to have a psychotic break or die does it), and it's not a bit overcast, so I should be able to scan the area.

I douse my night light and peel back the shade at the very corner.

My cousin Arlene is in the back yard. She's hunched over the breakfast room doorknob, seemingly trying to pick the lock.

At least I'm fairly sure it's Arlene. The last time I saw her she was plump and blonde. Typical cheerleader type, sixteen and happy. Confident in the knowledge that she'd be Waco High's Homecoming Queen—or at least in her court. But I know from my parents' supposedly secret conversations that she "turned bad" over the past year and started "running with the wrong crowd"; my Aunt Odile has been threatening to send her to a Catholic boarding school or one of those disciplinary boot camps, which she would never survive, any more than I could. Things stink for her at home.

But I definitely am not prepared to see this waiflike Goth washing up on our doorstep like some abandoned jellyfish tossed out of the aquarium for being too scary. Her hair is spiky-short, with bangs that come to a point over her nose like an inverted widow's peak, and it has been dyed a dull matte black like her clothing. Steel-toed work boots lace up around her calves. Overall, I'd rate her a ten in the Elvira look-alike contest. Except she totally lacks the wackily cheerful and appealing persona that the comic "Mistress of the Dark" projected. This is way more a Jane Eyre-drowning-in-the-sea vibe.

I shove the window upward. "Arlene! Up here," I call down as loudly as I dare. The wraithlike entity—evidently, it *is* Arlene—jumps back as if startled, then looks frantically heavenward. "Wait a minute, and I'll let you in."

I creep downstairs as quietly as a trayful of silverware falling down a metal duct, but no one shouts out, so I'm good. Yanking the door open, I get a good whiff of her and instinctively rear back. She and soap have been estranged for a while.

"Are you gonna let me in," she rasps out, stubbing out a cigarette on the sole of her boot. One of her $2500-orthodontia front teeth is chipped. My aunt must've died twenty-five hundred deaths over that.

"Sure." I take another step back, and she advances like a predator. It's like she's used to barging into places now, before they can change their minds about admitting her.

This is not the old Arlene. This Arlene is an apparition wearing full metal jacket armor—on the inside. Nervously I smooth my hair back and briefly hold it gathered until I realize I don't have a ponytail elastic and release it to cascade over my face. But through the veil of mousy hair I can still see the apparition, which looks extremely determined.

"What do y'all have to eat? I am absolutely starved, kiddo." She brushes past me, heading for the fridge.

The lights wink on overhead. June stomps in, rubbing her eyes. "What the f—" she begins, but then she sees Arlene. "—are you doing here?" she finishes, as if she'd meant to say that all along.

"That's about the size of it." Arlene scavenges among the leftovers, coming up with a cold chicken drumstick. She attacks it like a feaster at a Renaissance festival. My stomach feels hollow. "Turn the lights off," she says, squinting as if the light hurts her eyes.

June complies, throwing us back into the half-darkness of the night lights and the refrigerator bulb. Grabbing a loaf of bread, she loads the toaster and sets out butter and two kinds of jam. "You ran away?"

"Let's just say I have better things to do with my life than go to one of those torture camps. My parents do not own me like some cow in their pasture." My aunt and uncle have a cattle ranch near Waco "as an investment," although they live in town. "I am now liberated and making my own way." Arlene tosses her head, apparently forgetting the gesture wouldn't be dramatic, considering the current AWOL-ness of her cheerleader hair.

"I hear you. I can't wait to move out myself." June's voice is full of fake eagerness, but actually June is full of shit. She won't leave home until she's old enough for the retirement village. I know my sister. She enjoys living the parent-subsidized life way too much to go subsist in a garret. Or, more likely, in a trailer by the Interstate.

"You look like you're about ready to be on your own. You're getting a good figure," Arlene lies to my sister. She's currying favor for something. I just don't yet know what. But anyhow, June likes to hear how she's special, so she laps up the flattery.

I wish I had something special about me—like tiger-lily hair, purple eyes like Elizabeth Taylor had, or even freckles that form a map of Europe on my back. But I'm plain. Nothing special.

Except I'm smart and well read. Actually, I'm a sponge for ancient and useless information. My brain is like a pack of Trivial Pursuit cards flying in formation. I'm a fan of old movies and books, of antiquities (and by that I mean things known by my parents' generation as well as by the Egyptians, Greeks, and Romans), and of obscure factoids that can win game shows. My head is a continuously updating Wikipedia. However, that hardly counts for anything in today's world of surface beauty. It often works against me. Everything's all image with no need for substance. But I forget that and always expect more — usually too much, I guess.

Arlene is studying me, in a moment of (perplexing, to me) contemplation. She abruptly points at me. "You still do that math thing?"

The toast pops up, smoking, black on both sides. She eyes it avidly, her gaze on lockdown. June pulls a dinner knife out of the silverware drawer and starts scraping a piece for her.

I'd almost forgotten about that time I showed off "the math thing" for Arlene. I knew better, but I couldn't resist. My cheeks warm up. "Yeah, I guess."

"That's cool. People always want that." She seems to be musing to herself.

"Old Dumbsmart is taking accordion lessons, too." June hands her the scraped toast and a jar of strawberry jam.

"Oh, brother. That's one nobody'd ever want to buy." Then Arlene seems to realize that what she's saying doesn't make any sense and waves it away. "Anyway. You keep it up. Maybe it'll be worth something to somebody someday, who knows."

Arlene's upward-tilted nose means she always seems to be looking down her nose at you. June has this as well, but she doesn't give off the snobby effect so much, maybe because her face is so plump. They both look down their noses at me as they bite into their jamfests.

I've never understood people who can eat while smoking (or in the presence of anyone who is), but Arlene can do both at once. I'm hoping the cigarette odor will dissipate by the time Lynwood gets down here to start breakfast. I can't exactly open the back door in the middle of the night to fan the smoke out. Surreptitiously I switch on the Jenn-Aire's exhaust fan, but it doesn't seem to help much.

June gets the peanut butter out and starts making herself a sandwich. Arlene is licking grape jam off her fingers when Lynwood sweeps in, rubbing her eyes.

"*What* is going on down here at *four-thirty* in the *morning*? I can smell burned toast all the way upstairs." Lynwood flips on the overhead lights.

Arlene blinks innocently up at her, jam-handed (yet not ham-fisted), wreathed in a cloud of smoke, her head tilted, navy pea coat loose on her protruding collarbone. A moment's silence tells me it takes Lynwood that long to recognize her.

"Oh-Arlene-*honey*!" It pops out all one word as she rushes over to envelop my cousin in a hug. "I didn't expect…how did you…what are you doing here?"

It occurs to me that it's the better part of valor not to tell Arlene about the visit from the cops. I keep my mouth shut, and neither June nor Lynwood mentions it either. Arlene is adamant that we must not call her parents, that she's getting her head on straight and needs help from her favorite aunt. Said aunt falls for it, as always, whereas as a mother Lynwood gives no quarter.

"This will remain our little secret," Lynwood croons as she leads Arlene toward the back stairs, squeezing her around the shoulders. "We'll talk tomorrow. Now let's get you on up to bed. You can have June's room for the night, all to yourself."

June pokes me in the perma-bruise on my arm, as though it's my fault she doesn't get to double up with Vampyra.

Lynwood beams. "We'll discuss what you need in the morning, all righty?"

Once upstairs and left to our own devices, my sister and I gather in June's bedroom to watch Arlene get ready for bed. Or something. I'm not quite sure what. We're like groupies and she's the rock star, and we are waiting for enlightenment.

It comes in an unexpected form. Arlene doesn't say a word, but as we sit there we hear a knockdown-dragout shouting match begin between Gary and Lynwood about whether to call the cops (Gary's solution) or Arlene's parents (Lynwood's idea). Arlene seems oblivious.

She is sitting on the pink carpeting in June's bedroom sorting through her huge hobo purse and lighting up yet another nasty-smelling cigarette. June is still somewhat sulky about not getting to sleep in here at the guru's feet, but June will be fine on my bottom bunk. My room still has the old bunk beds we got at a garage sale when we first moved here; Lynwood painted them peach so I could have my Girl Scout friends over, except I quit the Scouts before I knew very many people and I never had those sleepovers.

Our cousin is mightily changed indeed. The old Arlene would've charged in here and started teaching us some new cheer ("Victory is our battle cry") or would've pulled out an Uno deck for a raucous game. Instead, she's counting out baggies of what looks like dried oregano but which I know must be pot, and sorting various evil-looking plastic containers with colored powders inside. She finishes and ties it all back up in a bandana that she shoves to the bottom of the purse.

"Shit," she explains with a heavy sigh.

For some reason, I don't think Arlene's a drug dealer. She's into something, that's for sure, but my intuition tells me she's dealing something a lot darker. This stuff is merely window-dressing.

June gapes at her. "So now that you're away from home, what do you do all day? I mean, you have a job now?"

My sister can be so clueless.

Arlene half-smiles. "I'm in sales, you might say. We buy and sell things people want and need." She flaps a hand nonchalantly. "Nothing illegal, of course." She grimaces at the thought. "Other things. Important things."

This sounds ominous. The word "nefarious" comes to mind, but I dismiss it as my instinctive paranoia. Still, my toes curl involuntarily.

She exhales smoke. "We're unique in our field. About to have a major breakthrough, and the world will hear from us. You can bet on it."

"That is so cool." June's eyes shine in the half-dark like a prowling tomcat's. It creeps me out.

Arlene is unbelievably worldly, and I realize that behind my sister's affectation of blasé knowingness, she is awed. That's what I mean about needing to watch out for June. It's kind of tiring, actually.

Finally the voices in our parents' room die down and a couple of slammed doors lead to quiet. June reaches up to douse the lamp, and the only light in the room is the glowing end of Arlene's ciggie. She stubs it out and fires up another with the flare of a sulfurous, old-fashioned wooden match. (Apparently she stashes them in the watch pocket of her jeans.)

In the dark, Arlene becomes expansive. "For old times' sake, let's do a visualization. I'll lead." She takes a deep drag and smoke forms a halo around her head. My eyes have adjusted to the faint moonlight through the window, and I can tell Arlene's eyes are glittering.

Why do I have an expanding feeling of unease?

Arlene reaches for the three-wicked candle June got for her birthday, the one she keeps on her nightstand. (She'd never dream of lighting it.) Another match fires all the wicks to flame, and a flickering eeriness fills the room. "Let us light the way for our spirits."

June eats this stuff up; she adores pretend games.

Ever since we were really little, Arlene has always played make-believe with us. You could really see things when Arlene got going and began to intone something unreal like, "We have landed on the planet Xmorth and now our spaceship glows pink like a ball of Play-Doh lava and transmits messages of peace to the gathering crowds as our staircase opens up and unfolds down into their waiting open arms." Under her spell, you believed six impossible things before lunchtime as she pulled you along in the red Radio Flyer or pushed you back and forth in the rusty swing with your eyes closed and your mind open so wide your brain sometimes flew out.

Arlene leads us in a hypnotic exploration with her sultry voice, as if she wields a cauldron and theremin, and for the moment I forget I'm lying on the pink bedroom carpet and truly believe I'm aboard a ship floating in a warm salty sea, surrounded by sea monsters and drifting ever closer to the Sirens who want to eat us and steal our talents.

At last Arlene's voice fades away as she evidently tires of us and the game. With a quick exhale she blows out the candle flames. "All right, come back to here and now. And then go away. I'm sleepy."

Our cousin still has that magic touch. In fact, she was so convincing that I'm still partly under her spell. June's eyes remain aglow with admiration and hero worship.

Somehow I drag June out of there after several reluctant "okay, goodnight" repetitions and get her settled in my room. Then I get nervous and (on the pretext that I have to tinkle) sneak back to make sure that Arlene has put out the cig. Instead I catch her hiding something behind the dresser drawer, the one that doesn't fit quite right, where June used to stash her fan fiction before she graduated to illicit cosmetics and music.

As they say, silence is golden, meaning it offers better odds for survival. I sneak quietly back to my bottom bunk without getting caught, wondering.

In the morning Arlene is gone.

June discovers her absence first, tearing around the house and yard at sunup, checking to make sure her idol has truly departed. She goes into her room and slams the door without saying anything to me.

Gary is the first to mention it at the breakfast table, where our usual parakeet-chatter has yielded to a somber silence. "Well, that solves our problem. Now we don't have to worry who we're betraying and why. She's gone on her merry way, and nobody needs to be any the wiser."

"But what's going to happen to her?" June says in a dangerously whine-like tone. I've seldom seen her show such concern for anybody, short of the sexy Justin Fink.

"She'll be fine." Gary watches his eggs staring up at him and pinions them with a fork, as if they might slither off the plate.

"She's only a child." Lynwood swirls her spoon in her iced tea glass until it rings.

"She looked like a perfectly capable grown-up woman to me," Gary says darkly. When did he glimpse her? I don't like the look in his eyes.

"What if the cops come back?" June ventures to ask in a mild, nonchalant tone, but I feel the tension crackling beneath the surface of her question.

"Then we have to tell them she was here." He shrugs. "I'm not putting my family on the line just to keep her on the streets instead of back home where she belongs."

"We can't turn her in. I know my sister, and I'm certain they're not being fair to Arlene at home." Lynwood's lower lip pops out; it looks exactly like June's does when she pouts.

Apparently, Arlene is a Major Sinner. She has (allegedly) stolen money from her dad's cookie jar, and was (supposedly) caught in *flagrante delicto* by her mother with some new boyfriend they don't care for. Then, they claim, she got in with the druggie crowd and somebody was killed over a deal that went bad, and that's theoretically why the police are sniffing around for Arlene, to question her. All of this is hearsay, I want to remind them, but I do have the sense to keep quiet.

"Maybe she should go to Toughlove Camp and get straightened out," Gary says, in what some might assume is a reasonable tone.

"My God," Lynwood squeaks, her voice taking on a hint of hysteria. "I've read about those horrid places. The articles say that untrained guards run roughshod over defenseless children, ignoring their injuries and beating them for hiccupping. It's completely out of the question. We have to protect her any way we can. I only wish she had confided in me before all this happened."

The argument escalates until Gary throws his napkin over his uneaten eggs (they do stare up at you something awful) and slams out of the house. If this were a movie, he'd be going to a bar, but since it's him I expect he's just running to SuperAceTruValu Hardware, where he will pick up a few light bulbs before slinking quietly home through the back door.

With all the distractions, I almost don't notice that June keeps her left hand hidden under the table through all this.

June and I are chilling in the treehouse when a yellow Hummer pulls up across the street. After scrutinizing it through the telescope, June announces that she's going out front to get the mail. I scramble down the rope ladder after her, because she has no interest in the daily post (unless she has ordered one of those breast-enhancing exercisers again), so of course she's up to something.

Up close, the Hummer's driver is a James Dean clone: dark glasses, white tee with cigarette pack rolled up in one sleeve, faded Levi's tucked into Frye motorcycle boots, blond hair slicked straight back in a ducktail but with one unruly forelock that flips over his right temple. I didn't know June went for that type, but she seems duly impressed.

The guy acts happy to see us. He says he is Arlene's boyfriend. I have my doubts, because when I challenge him he "doesn't remember" her favorite color, puce, nor her fave musical group, which I know is still Deathtöngue.

I persist. "What's your name? I'm sure she would've mentioned you."

He dismisses me with a sour look and turns his charm (ha) on June. When he suggests we go for a little ride, I tell June we shouldn't go, but she says, "Nonsense," and jumps into his cadmium yellow deathtrap.

I cannot let her go alone, and I have never ridden in a Hummer. So after a moment I hop into the back with a prayer that we aren't found dead in a field next week. Or tomorrow.

All he wants, it turns out, is to cruise the neighborhood while cross-examining us about Arlene.

June is all too happy to oblige. She's usually too sharp to fall for this kind of thing, but they're together in the front seat and he's flirting with her and pinching the ends of her hair and stroking her cheek so that she is completely lost in him, whereas I keep my head about me and remain adamantly circumspect (to put it in terms that Lynwood and the SAT Word of the Day Committee would applaud.) I'm hoping they'll forget I'm back here.

He keeps asking, "Did she leave anything with you? Give you something for safekeeping?"

Of course I flash on whatever it was I saw Arlene hide, but I keep my expression passive and do the slackjawed kid act and he doesn't pay me no never mind, which for once is a Good Thing.

June plays the little fool, blathering on about this and that. And I get a look at what she was hiding at breakfast.

Apparently Arlene slipped June a ring to keep for her at some point when I wasn't looking. Furthermore, although she didn't trust her own sister with it, the bad boy persuades her to take it off her finger and hand it over. He duly examines it, but it's nothing but a dull old piece of junk, without even a stone, just the end of a spoon handle bent around into an adjustable loop, and he can see it's tarnished and scratched, so he hands it back and squints. "Anything else?"

"No, nothing else. Hee hee," says June, and I realize she is tilting her head coquettishly because she's trying to flirt. Oh, spare me. This jerk has no finesse, no charisma; he must get by on a combination of native charm and base cunning. I didn't know that smarminess would blow June's skirts over her head.

They go into the sort of dull banter you hear in direct-to-disc movies as he drives aimlessly. I honestly think they have forgotten I'm back here.

Eventually he parks at the edge of our development's landscaped greenspace-slash-play-area. A short time later, a police car pulls up beside us. Before Darkman can hit the ignition, there's an officer next to his window.

"Step out of the car, please," the officer says to him, fingering his nightstick or baton or whatever those things are. (They're fairly awe-inspiring up close.)

The guy is old enough to know that the cops always check you out if they think you are "parking," meaning making out, even if you're only in a deep philosophical discussion. And he ought to have realized that cops routinely patrol fancy neighborhoods like ours. One of our busybody neighbors probably called in a "suspicious vehicle" because of our aimless prowling, and the cops ran the plates. A grown man should've known better than to park near a swing set in a showy ride containing two minor females.

Next thing I know June and I are riding home in a cop car. June leans forward asking the officer questions about stakeouts and police work she's seen on television, not bothering to hide her enthusiasm, but I'm panicky. My fingernails dig dents into my palms. I hate being on the other side of the chicken wire, even though we're only getting a courtesy ride home so the police can scold our parents.

Sure enough, the officer lectures Lynwood when she answers the door. "You need to keep a better eye on your daughters, ma'am. They were found associating with a known felon."

A felon! June's gaze searches out mine and we both goggle. I can see she's turned on by the idea. Great.

Good thing I've been studying all those synonyms for the SAT vocabulary section. Felon? Try ruffian, blackguard, rogue. Those are far more entertaining terms than punk, thug, or hooligan for such a person.

Although what seems odd is that even with the police visit, I *still* didn't catch the guy's name.

Lynwood is hysterical. "You know better than to go off with a strange boy."

"He's Arlene's boyfriend, Mother," says June, dropping effortlessly into Arlene's coolly sarcastic tone, and I suddenly know she is changing. My sister is Becoming A Woman. Soon she'll be like Arlene and start drawing away from me. I can feel the gulf between us opening up like an abyss and I stare down at my shoes, terrified.

Lynwood's voice in my ear brings me back. "What about you, April? You knew better. You should have run home, and we could've had your sister rescued."

I try to play the Arlene card. "Motherrr!" But it doesn't work for me any better than your average nun can shinny up a stripper pole, and I end up whining. "I couldn't let her go off alone and there just wasn't time to come get you."

"You could have called on your cell phone."

The thought hadn't entered my mind. But I lied. "Battery's dead."

"Well, you'll have plenty of time to charge it."

We are grounded. Possibly forever.

books can be deceiving

June does not take discipline well. She stomps off
to the treehouse (we're allowed to stay inside the fence
only) with the magazines she got the last time we went to
the drugstore, an eclectic collection of *How To Get A Teen-
age Boy And What To Do With Him Once You Get Him*-type
advice zines and music fan stuff in the vein of *Tiger Beat*.
Possibly a biker mag in the mix somewhere. She drags me
out there (thumb on perma-bruise) to show me what I
should be wearing from now on, all of which is lace-up
leather with predrilled, grommeted holes.

Gross. Just looking at that stuff makes me glad that I
could probably squirm out of bondage leathers if I had

to. That's because my right shoulder is double-jointed, which means I can change its position and wriggle out of someone's grip. Sometimes. Sometimes not. And sometimes the joint bothers me. Today it's kind of bugging me.

June soon loses interest in schooling me and turns to her usual pursuit of scanning the neighborhood for interesting action.

I flop down on my old bean bag chair. It's orange vinyl where June's is purple, and it leaks Styrofoam pellets that cling to you like butt dandruff. I could set up my laptop here and do some history; there's an online quiz I'm fairly sure I'm ready for. American Civil War 1861–1865 and that "O Captain" poem. WiFi strength is good enough for me to connect from here. I should do this.

But coursework can't hold my attention.

June is sitting on a stack of Lynwood's silk pillows that didn't quite match the watered silk sofa, but I decide not to ask whether she got permission to bring them out here where they're squashed down against raw boards. The treehouse is very basic, but it's on a hill in the backyard, which is why we can see into other yards and spy on every front door halfway down the street. For me, though, peeping has gotten old. I never did feel right about it, anyway.

When my sister swivels the scope to start spying on Mr. Feenster at his home computer (Justin is taking a well-deserved break from roasting himself), I say I need to go to the bathroom. She doesn't answer me, nor does she seem to notice me climbing down the rope netting that serves as a ladder and heading for the house — and, ostensibly, our shared bath.

Instead, I sneak into June's room and pull out the bottom dresser drawer.

In the hidey-hole is a book.

Arlene reads?

The crinkled black leather cover makes me think of an old family Bible or some valuable first edition. In fact, I wonder how it has stayed in such good shape, as ancient as it seems to be. No cracks or tears in the binding. I believe it's leather, even though it feels cushy, a little like microfiber, or that fake suede they use to make jackets.

The book is cold to the touch as I turn it over in my hands, which is weird because it has been cozy behind the drawer where no breeze could reach it. It smells musty, as if it has been waiting in the stacks of an old library.

Inside, it has blank pages like a sketchbook. Paging back and forth reveals no markings on the ivory paper. As I stare at the first page, a drawing appears of me and June in the treehouse, watching through the telescope as the cops drive away with Arlene's alleged boyfriend.

That makes me blink. How could the drawing *fade in* (that's the only way I can describe it, the opposite of fading out) as I watch? I must've just missed it originally. Right?

But I realize it's not a charcoal drawing as I had first thought, but a colored-pencil sketch, done by a fairly accomplished artist. With some really good details that make me certain it's our treehouse—including my old red high-tops sitting in the corner by June's stack of magazines. Which is plain eerie. June just carried those magazines out a little while earlier…so how could the artist have known they were going to be there? Also, how could Arlene have drawn this? She can't draw flies.

"April?" Gary's voice, right behind me. I slam the book.

He takes one look at the drawer and its contents spilled at my feet, his gaze targeting the book. "You're snooping in your sister's room, and you know better. Is that your sister's diary?"

I roll my eyes. "Her diary is on her laptop," I point out helpfully, "and it's encrypted using Stage 2 Satori and has two passwords. The NSA would have difficulty getting into it."

"April," he says in a tone of warning. "You know what I mean. What is that book you have? Something she felt she had to hide?"

With an ominous Sense of Purpose, he reaches around to snatch the possible porn out of my hands. But then he looks at the first few pages of the book he has grabbed and says, "Oh," like he's confused. He thumb-flips through a few pages. "I loved this as a kid. Why would you two be hiding this?"

He's waving it around as if it's a long-lost book from his childhood. No mention of the drawing or of the blank pages. Is he trying to make me doubt my senses? In a moment it becomes obvious that he's completely unhinged. Apparently, he thinks it's a novel.

This is a Good Thing. Keep in mind that when Gary says, "It's Miller time," he means Henry Miller. The writer. Dirty old man writer, if you ask me. Although of course we are not allowed to read him "until college," Gary warns with a waggling index finger. If you want to read porn, I always say, you ought to go for the best, and Miller's reportedly the best perv writer around. And as far as the Great American Novel goes, Gary could reel off at least ten candidates and give you the reasoning behind his choices, if you let him. Anyway, my *point* is that Gary is way into literature and the classics.

I am saved.

He beams down at the book. "My old copy of Howard Pyle's *Adventures of Robin Hood*. Why would your sister keep this hidden behind her drawer?"

He knew about June's secret hiding place all along, of course. I should've known.

I blink innocently. "I guess she doesn't want me to read it."

He shoots me a look that's supposed to let me know he's on to me. "The cover is the same one that was on my old book. Must be a reproduction." He thinks the book cover is some old-timey painting?

He finally waves the book in the air, grinning. "Let's get her drawer put back like it was. But you tell her that I said you should both read this. It's practically a family heirloom." He shakes his head. "She doesn't have to hide *books* from us, for goodness' sake. Certainly not this one. I know you'll take good care of it. Have you ever damaged or destroyed one of her books?"

"Of course not." I haven't; I never dog-ear pages or even lay one on its face to keep my place. I am the original dead-tree-book preserver and defender. I'm obsessive.

"Well, then. You two each read this and do me a book report. It's a classic." He's perfectly serious; I can tell. I've lived here all my life and I know this man.

I manage a weak smile. The book is still a blank tome bound in black leather. He's either testing me or he's crazy. Probably both.

By this time I know that June must be suspicious. It's about time for her to come find me. Sure enough, her face appears in the mirror behind my head like an apparition.

"What are you two doing in MY ROOM?" she shrieks.

Gary pats her shoulder. "Just talking, sweetheart. Your sister's going to read this on my recommendation, and you don't have to hide it. You never have to hide great literature from us. Well, you girls keep getting along now." With a smile he begins humming a tune, one that is somehow familiar, yet I can't quite place it; it's some old jazz standard. He practically skips down the bedroom hall like Happy Bunny, probably thinking of how literary his children are.

June marches over and snatches the book out of my hands. In preparation, she levers her thumb over my perma-bruise. "What was that all about and what is he talking about? Oh…." She looks confused and flips through the pages bemusedly. Her grip on my arm loosens. "I thought you had something of mine. I can't believe you kept a babyish book like this one. Even the cover is a cartoon, and it looks nothing like an ark. I'd have thought you'd read the King James, or at least some respectable translation." From the way she talks, she seemingly thinks it's the Children's Bible that I won in Vacation Bible School years ago as an award, stuffed with various award ribbons that they gave me and tracts that I saved.

"How do you know what Noah's ark looked like?"

She snorts and tosses the book at me, and I clutch it as it bangs into my chest. "What were you doing in here?"

"You know Gary. Just nosing around, trying to get me to reveal your hiding places and all your secrets. Don't worry—I didn't."

For some reason, she buys this and I don't get punched. "Who can ever understand that man?" She turns to go, but thinks better of it. "You may precede me out," she says, turning back. "Bring that book with you. Don't leave your junk in my room."

So neither one of them saw the book as it is, but as... what? A book they wanted it to be? What it wanted them to see?

Something's way fishy about this. I evaluate the chances that they are in cahoots to make me crazy. Probability is, in reality, fairly low.

Perhaps (duh) there is something odd about the book itself (ouch, bruised by the clue stick.)

I test this theory by carrying the book into the kitchen where Lynwood is making some kind of low-fat no-carb lunch out of dust and vitamins. Setting it down on the countertop next to her work area, I wait for her to snatch it up because "library books have so many germs."

True to form, she does. "Don't put things where I'm cooking." Then she frowned, looking confused. "Oh, look at this...aw. How sweet. I had to read this in school. I know it's boring at first, but stick with it and it'll reward you. I can't believe you are already reading into the ninth-grade language arts list. You are such a good student."

She evidently thinks it's a book out of our school reading list.

I give her my best Miss Priss smile like that mean blonde girl out of *Little Whorehouse on the Prairie* and simper forth with, "I want to read all the ninth grade books this semester and get ahead so I can do Early Decision admission to Stanford. I finished the eighth grade list last month." That much is actually true.

That really pushes Lynwood's button, as Stanford is her alma mater. She beams. "Super! That's my April." Forgetting that I'm supposed to be on a low-sugar regimen (she read something about yeast proliferation and the anti-Candida diet to control it, and decided she'd put me on it to see what happened, not because I'm fat like June), she cuts me a brownie—the health food version, of course. "Run along and read."

The brownie is made of organic dust and a new artificial sweetener. After one bite I ditch it in a potted plant that I'll probably find wilted tomorrow. I retreat to my room to contemplate what this double-crossing tome actually is.

Pro'lly something of the Devil.

I decide to open it again anyway.

I'll admit, my hands are shaking a little. And those bongos I hear are actually my own heartbeats. Could the spidery branches in the outer corner of each eye be from stress?

But I'm brave. I flip the book open as if it's nothing more than a Chinese restaurant menu.

It has changed. Into a blank journal with rainbow pages: the first is pink, the next is yellow, etc. But the image I saw earlier isn't there now. All the pages are clean.

A couple of years ago, June went through a big swords-and-sorcery phase. She got hooked on the first of the Harry Potter books and, after consuming them at an alarming rate, graduated to Narnia, Middle-Earth, and the Conan oeuvre (all easily available from the local used book store). The first time Gary found one of her paperbacks (an old classic by either Fritz Leiber or Robert E. Howard, with a cover featuring a tunic-clad barbarian holding a jeweled sword over a multi-headed beast while a buxom maiden cowered underneath), he almost split a gut. He guided June away from "historical" fiction and toward modern fantasy. Turning to film, she spent hours watching all the witchy movies she could find, starting with *Bell, Book, and Candle*, and ending with *The Craft* (which is dang scary, and I know, because I watched it with her.)

So the idea of magic is nothing new to me. Books have always seemed at least part magic because of the way they let you visualize things that never happened while you take a tour of someone's mind, someone you will probably never meet and who may already have crossed that eternal Veil. I have even suspected that a few events we've called happy coincidences were really some sort of deep earth magic responding to our inner needs and desires. Magic, I believe, has as much right to exist as science.

Still, I didn't expect it to burst forth into my own reality quite so insistently.

I flip a few more pages back and forth and watch as they all fade to black. Solid stone pitch black. The lights are out and no one's home.

Apparently the book has nothing to say to me at the moment.

Thinking better of slamming the pages shut, I gently tap the front cover back down. It looks satisfied. (I know I'm personifying an inanimate object. The truth, though, is that the book seems to radiate self-satisfaction like an aura. Perhaps it thinks it's got me going, that I'm scared. At least marginally, ha ha, shaken. Am I?)

I like to think of myself as a go-with-the-flow type who isn't easily rattled by anything. Okay, here's a cute guy, flirt a little; hey, I've just time-traveled 200 years into the future, this could be interesting, let's find a flying car; wait, this book is actually a magical grimoire with powers; cool, what's next?

But I'm actually nothing like that. I'm kind of the opposite of "unflappable" ("flappable"? Not an SAT word, at least not with this meaning.) Even Gary says I sometimes overthink things (but if you think about it, how can you "overthink" something? It's impossible to over-analyze. If anything, people don't think deeply *enough*, if you ask me.)

I need time to process this. Obviously, the book has an advantage in that it knows what—or who—I am, but I have no idea (yet) who or what *it* may be. Well, maybe it has given me a hint, but until it's ready to be more forthcoming, I'll have to wait.

So I secrete it away, finding a great hiding place in my own room, and then head back outside to see what June is doing in the treehouse.

hair today

June has black rings around her eyes.

Of course, I have to ask. "Whoa. What's that all over your face?"

She grabs a cracked old hand mirror of Lynwood's and glances in before she realizes how dumb I am. "Cru, you idiot. It's makeup."

She has on black eyeliner about an inch wide. She doesn't look at all like Arlene, though. She looks as if she's been pranked with one of those pairs of trick binoculars.

"Well, I don't think it looks good."

She rolls her raccoon eyes. "That's *your* opinion," she says, leaving no doubt about what she thinks of its value.

Turning away from me, she continues to count out the change from our huge plastic Dallas Cowboys bank we got at the State Fair when I was nine. It's in the shape of a beer bottle, complete with bottle cap. We must have a thousand dollars in dimes and quarters in there, or we would if they were dimes and quarters, but it's mostly pennies. She's sorting out the silver.

"What are you doing?" Immediately, I wince. What I mean is, "what are you going to buy," but I have opened the door for a smart-assed retort. When will I become quick-witted like June?

She doesn't even look up. "I think I have enough. C'mon, if you want to tag along with me to Wacker's."

"We're grounded."

She shoots me a withering look. It means: What parents don't know won't hurt them, and ours are already occupied again with their own pursuits. They'll never check on us.

I follow her down the rope ladder and onto our bicycles. Mine is a yellow BMX in great condition that Lynwood got at a garage sale, but June's came from an expensive bike shop and is almost worn out already.

It'd be nice in one sense if June were old enough to drive, but in another way I dread that day. She'll jump into the extra car, Lynwood's old Green Hornet, and speed away. And I'll probably never see her again.

Wacker's is a dollar store that looks the same as it did in the sixties when it was a classic five-and-dime (they never took down the old sign). Dollar stores are today's five-and-dimes, according to Gary, who praises God for them whenever Lynwood needs cheap-but-nice ceramic cat vases or similar gifties for clients.

The speckled linoleum floor tiles are cracked, and the dirt between them probably goes all the way to China. It reeks of Murphy's Oil Soap (proving that someone at least tries to clean the place now and then) and the incense sticks they sell at the checkout counter (Mystic Indian Incense, patchouli or sagebrush). We breeze directly to the cosmetics aisle. I start to reach for a pair of false lashes, thinking June's just going for the painted-tart look, but then I realize she's going for the full Arlene. Because she's sorting through boxes of hair dye. Black.

"Raven," she reads off the back of a battered box. "Ebony. How do you tell...?"

"There's a nylon swatch on the shelf." I know this because Lynwood used to dye her hair Mercurochrome-color when maroon heads were all the rage. "Except it shows what your hair would look like if it got bleached completely white before you dyed it. So you might not get exactly that shade."

My sister looks shocked that I know anything useful. She brandishes *Deep Ebony.* "This one is fine."

"What are you going to—" I stop myself before I ask YASQ (Yet Another Stupid Question) and change it to my real question, "Why?" We both have mouse-toned hair in a sort of no-style style that used to be a Buster Brown-type bob, but which is now kind of a nondescript pageboy-flip, depending on how recently I've combed it. I usually wear mine in a ponytail, or like Alice in Wonderland with half of it up now that it's finally gotten long enough, just past my shoulders. But June does a lot of upsweeps and braids using the BeautyBraids book Lynwood gave us years ago when that was popular. Who needs the upkeep of matte-black Goth hair?

But apparently June has fallen prey to the Arlene monster. She heads for the checkout and is contemplating which candy bar she'll get as I stand there waiting like a turkey drowning in the rain. Spoon ring flashing on her thumb, she counts out the change onto the countertop. Then she heads for the door.

I start to follow and run headlong into a tall, lean hunk barging in through the exit-only door.

It's Justin Fink. He smiles. "Hey, April. Lookin' good. What're you buying?"

"Um." My hand shoots out on its own and grabs a cola-flavored lip gloss off a hook near the register. I hold it up, but words won't form in my dehydrated mouth.

He winks. "Good choice. I love the taste of that stuff. I mean, on girls." With a toss of his shaggy dark hair he turns and heads down towards the auto parts aisle.

For some reason, I have not fainted. Yet. Justin is flirting with me? He likes me? *That* way?

The clerk is giving me a hard stare. "That be all?"

I snatch up some cinnamon gum and slap it down for her to ring up along with my gloss. I'm not a fan of candy bars—it's true, I don't like chocolate, and yes, I know there's something wrong with me. June thinks there's a sort of bitterness that's built into my saliva so it freaks up my taste buds. I used to eat SweeTarts and acidic Sour Patch Bears and Smartees (which June calls Dumbees) until I got tired of having all the skin peel off the roof of my mouth.

It's easy to catch up with June. Unlike in other things, June is a slow pedaler, and I'm pretty good on a bike. Especially when I'm floating, Justin-hello-powered. I'm also fairly decent on the climbing wall at Indoor Canyons Athletics, but I've never gotten quite this high solely on endorphins.

When we get home, I can sense the Tower is about to fall.

June commandeers the upstairs bath that connects our two bedrooms. She locks the doors—not just to the bathroom, but also the doors to both our bedrooms. If Lynwood or Gary should come up here, we're in for it over the locked doors, as there is a rule in our house that one never locks one's bedroom door, on the theory that we might be choking to death or having a séance. June does it anyway, to give her advance warning of the beatings to ensue.

She spreads out all of Lynwood's white towels across the countertop. White on the theory that "they'll bleach out fine." I am thinking that they'll bleach up to a spotty gray at best and that we should use the old, worn-out dark blue ones and then throw them out and play dumb if and when we're asked what happened to them. June, as always, gets her way and proceeds heedlessly on to mix the Super Secret Solution.

"Gag," I croak out, throwing open the window. "That stinks."

"You don't have to be in here," she says, rationally enough. But I am the kind of person who likes to watch a pair of locomotives rushing at one another and say, "Oh no oh no oh no," without being able to do anything to prevent the train wreck.

"You're supposed to have the plastic gloves on already." I peel them off the reverse of the unread instruction sheet. "And you'd better take off that silver ring first. The fumes alone might turn it black."

This stands to reason, but she shoots me a murderous look. Still, she slips the ring off—actually, she tugs on it and then she pulls harder and then she winces and finally she twists the ring rather viciously. It slips off her swollen flesh with effort, and she secretes it somewhere on her person.

If it's too tight, she ought to adjust it.

Staring down at the imposingly dark tube of crème, I try again to figure out June's voluntary act of self-uglification. Lynwood likes only blonde children. In this respect she's like the Queen Bee, forties actress Joan Crawford, who reputedly also said that. We have been a disappointment to her since the onset of puberty and the accompanying darkening of our towhead locks. Ever since, she has constantly been after us to let her bleach our hair. I never wanted to be a phony, while June was just being contrary when she said she liked the color of dead leaves.

I don't have any idea what Lynwood's reaction is going to be. She wouldn't let June shave her head last year during her "rapper" phase, either, which is the only way I can imagine getting rid of this industrial-strength dye.

The ammonia fumes are choking me and I hang my head out the window, meaning I have to pop the screen out and let it land on the grass in the front yard. If the fumes get too bad, we can drop the fire escape ladder Lynwood has stowed in the linen closet. I've always wanted to try it out.

Whoa. There's Arlene's "boyfriend" (or whoever he really is) again, sitting at the end of the block, but he isn't in the Hummer. There's no way he could be inconspicuous in that thing, and of course now the heat is on to him. But why he is parked at the curb in a blue Chevrolet Landbarge, a real junker, is pondersome.

I do not personally believe that he is at all interested in my sister, although it may serve his purposes to have her believe that. It's probable that he's keeping surveillance on us—surveilling?—to see if Arlene comes back. She must've dumped him really hard.

I think he sees me. Oops.

Feeling like Harriet the Spy, I pull my head back in to see a completely ridiculous-looking June, with her hair piled on top of her head all sticky and purple. Her skin is so pale that this contrast will make her look like an albino wearing a Beatles mop. But I suppose that's the point.

She holds up a pair of scissors she found in the drawer and thrusts them towards me. "I've decided to cut bangs. But I don't want to mess up, so you do it." She pinches a wad of hair from her front hairline and twists it, then runs the twisted strands down her nose. "I read in *Hair Today, Gone Tomorrow* magazine that if you cut at the end of your nose, they'll be the right length."

I don't think bangs are a good idea at all, considering how long it took to grow ours out last time and how bad her porcine face had looked with them. But, of course, Arlene has them.

This is definitely going to end badly.

I grab the shears. But for once, I shake my head. "Not while that goop is in there. Finish the dye job first and then I might think about it. That gunk is running down your forehead, by the way." Behind my back, I dangle them out the open window. They can't do any more damage landing in the grass than they will in here.

"I don't care. Give me those." She starts dancing the keep-away with me just as the pounding begins. It's both Gary and Lynwood, one per bedroom door.

Lynwood's voice is reedy and strained. "What are you girls up to? There's a terrible smell coming through the air vents." We have the house's expensive air-handling system to thank for our betrayal.

"This door is locked! Are you all right?" I can hear Gary rattling the knob a split second before the door to June's room pops open.

Apparently Gary has gotten a key made.

We look at each other. I shove the scissors back into a drawer just as the bathroom doorknob yields and the door slams flat against the wall. An incredulous Gary stands there goggling.

"We thought the house was on fire," screeches Lynwood from just over his shoulder. She heard him getting in and circled back, I guess. Her eyes are kind of wild. I suppose she might have thought that, as it does smell like burning hair in here. Although burning hair smells very little like burning house. June gets her tendency to exaggerate from Lynwood.

"You girls shouldn't sneak around and lock doors. You're young and you don't realize the dangers of— things," Gary begins.

It crosses my mind that they must've thought we were cooking up some crystal meth or doing something equally nightmarish. They appear to be entirely clueless and even (maybe) a bit disappointed at the letdown. (Okay, that could be my imagination.)

Then the situation registers. "Oh, my God. What have you done to yourself?" Lynwood screeches.

The dye has been setting for long enough that Lynwood can't just wash it out and expect no effect. Yet Lynwood marches my sister into the tub and turns on the shower, heedless of the fact that June's wearing her best jeans. "Get out," she commands us, and Gary retreats as if he'd been caught peeping. I am on his heels.

Evil cursings ensue behind the door as she and June go at it. I don't think even Gary's special dandruff shampoo is going to take that color out.

Downstairs in the kitchen, we land at the breakfast bar as if we're at Waffle House about to order two Rip-Roarin' Pancake Platters. We regard each other warily.

Gary asks me in a subdued voice, "Does she really think matte raven hair will look good on her? Or is she doing it for some other reason?"

I look at him blankly. Everyone always has a reason for what he or she does, and June has an elaborate rationale for most of her actions, but in this endeavor she had given me no explanation at all. However, it would be fairly obvious to any woman what was going on. I have to feel sorry for Gary, because after all he *is* the only guy in this household.

When I don't answer, he prompts me. "For a boy? Because of her peer group? To join a gang?"

I laugh out loud.

He frowns. "Okay, I know she's not a joiner."

He's got that right.

I'm not about to share with him how alarmed I am. I don't like the direction this is heading. I mean, with my sister Growing Up and Rebelling all of a sudden. Yes, I knew it would happen someday. But I think the situation is accelerating, and it's all related to that ring from Arlene and the guy who keeps showing up trying to steal it, and that's what really makes me nervous. Of course I can't say to Gary that I think my sister is coming under the influence of witches or magicians or whatever, unless I want to be fitted for one of those jackets with the long sleeves that buckle together in back.

What I need to do is go study that book some more, although I don't think I'll get a chance again for a while. It's got to hold some answers for me. Of course, this could just be June's hormones, nothing more. I could be reading too much into it.

"It's normal," I tell him in the most nonchalant tone I can manage. "Like, she's turning into a typical teen." I shrug. Surely he can figure it out; he is smart. "You know. Like on MTV."

"Oh, God." His elbows land on the countertop and he drops his face into his hands.

I feel kind of sorry for him. And for me.

goon tomorrow

Lynwood takes us both to her hairdresser, Lancelot.

"He works wonders. I've already phoned and he knows what I want. It's great that he had two appointments open in a row; you look shaggy," she tells me as June climbs haughtily out of the BMW.

I don't really want anything crazy done to my hair. It's finally long enough to look halfway decent in a ponytail instead of like a horse whose tail was stolen by bandits, and if it were up to me I would just keep it longish and straight and visit the local SuperChops for a minimal maintenance trim every couple of months or so.

But you don't argue with Lynwood when she talks of Keeping You In Fashion, so I get out of the car.

Lynwood isn't coming in with us; the salon is close to the Galleria and she wants to pop into NeedlessMarkup for a cosmetics update. "See you in a couple of hours. Be good."

She gives June the credit card, so I know that if June has a mind to, she'll buy shampoo and nail polish and for all I know we'll emerge with shiny fingertips and toes. That's all right, as I feel a bit rebellious myself. I shouldn't get in trouble solely for being an accomplice.

All makeup has been scrubbed off and June is back to normal, if a bit paler than usual. I mean, in the face, because her hair definitely isn't. The coal tar has done its work magnificently.

Lance-a-roo is aghast. "So you're going to join the Emo movement? It's quite out of date now." He clucks and hands her immediately off to his colorist. I am duly wet down and lounge on the all-metal torture rack they call a sofa to page through dingbat magazines ("Ten Most Wanted Midlength Styles") until he waves me into his evil chair of havoc-wreaking.

He's waiflike, perhaps even wispy, six feet and anorexic, contact-lens-turquoise eyes huge in his thin face. I catch a whiff of Davedevil cologne, the one advertised by the newest teen idol. He pinches up a strand of my cringing hair and lets it fall like a limp, overcooked piece of spaghetti. "*Qu'est-ce que c'est?*" he says in a wondering tone.

That's French for "what is this?" (as Lynwood loves to point out when she says it), but there's so much more implied in the way Lance vocalizes it.

I agree to a "trim"—or what he considers a trim—bringing my hair "up" (they euphemistically say "bringing it up," although they are chopping it *off*) to the bottom of my earlobes, exposing the back of my neck to the cold. I squeeze my eyes closed, but I can still feel him working away, whistling some tuneless sonata. "Too bad you don't have enough to donate, but we're not going to let this get that far out of hand, are we?" he chirps.

I have to wonder: did Rapunzel donate? In today's society, that would be the most important question people would ask her.

He does on me the A-line style that Lynwood wears these days, where the front of the bob is longer than the back. And shingled. You know, hacked up the back of the neck as if you were attacked by a weed-whacker. I hope Justin won't think I'm ruined. No bangs, at least.

I don't look like myself when he gets through with his blowout and shine serum. I hate it, but then I hate all haircuts. I hate change.

June marches back in looking dipped in Clorox. Her locks are as white as that albino guy's, the one who's the villain in that weird movie, and her face is only a couple of Pantone shades darker. Lance claps his hands and pronounces her hair "fried, dyed, and refried." He rubs a few strands between his fingers as if he expects them to turn to dust. Fairy dust, I suppose. She sure needs some.

June's hands flutter to her head, the glowing silver ring restored to its proper place on her thumb and sparkling wildly in the beams of the salon's pinpoint halogen track lights. Then she leans close to him and says in conspiratorial tones, "I brought a picture. Lynwood told you, didn't she?"

"About what?" But he is a hair artist and they all have a cutting fetish (why else would they choose a profession where they stand on their feet and hold their arms out for hours every day?), so when June produces a photo out of her pocket his eyes flash four colors, even brighter than the spoon ring. "Of course that will be *darling* on you, darling."

I close my eyes. When I open them again, he has all of her hair gathered into a rope at the top of her head like Pebbles Flintstone's and half the salon is counting down. "Three, two, one," and he saws through it and June is…bald! Practically.

It is the 1971 Liza Minnelli Gamine, the Mia Farrow *Rosemary's Baby* look, and the newest Miley Cyrus-inspired craze, I suppose. June certainly looks waifish, if you like fat waifs. Her head is a cantaloupe with eyes. But the staff is gathering around, and they break into choreographed applause. My sister loves being the center of attention, if it's approval, and she is wreathed in smiles.

The sadist cuts even more, making a spiky-looking fringe of bangs (I sigh) and a very uneven bottom line. I thought the point of a haircut was to even up that line, but everyone else is full of praise. Clients and stylists alike rush across the salon to applaud her courage and decisiveness. Her teeth and ring sparkle in the limelight.

Her gaze hits me, her eyes silently asking, *If they say it is good, it must be good, right?*

I smile weakly and nod. June's drive to transform has gone into overdrive, which surely bodes nothing good. Next we'll be discussing what we might do in order to attract the proper kind of dude. I am terrified by the thought. Although I'll admit that I'm jonesing for Justin.

But it's mostly a fantasy. If he kissed me, I'd probably flatline.

Lynwood's Beemer sails right by us the first time.

She circles the block and passes us again, incredibly. Then she throws it into reverse, screeches to a halt just short of my toes, and pops out like a pastry leaping out of the toaster because it has suddenly realized it's melting. "Aieeee!"

Lynwood shrieks again as she grabs June by her upper arms and shakes her, fairly hard. Then she marches June into the salon to Have A Word. It only takes a minute for them to troop back out, though, June smirking triumphantly and Lynwood looking mollified. Lance has worked his charms on our mother. I'll bet Lynwood would've retrieved June's discarded hair if she could have found it, though, for her baby book.

"I want to stop at Nordstrom," June announces. "For a makeup consultation."

Lynwood has just had a consultation, judging from the new paint on her cheeks and eyelids and the dinky bag of tiny samples (vials with one fingertip-ful of each new potion they're promoting). But we pull a U-ie and head to the mall. She wants to encourage any signs of fashionableness in us, as we usually knock around the treehouse and our rooms in jeans and tees. She probably does a novena now and then for our style enlightenment.

I hope I'm only along for the ride.

After hearing how fantastic her now-approved new look is from all the Nerdstrom and Needless Markup clerks, June gets a teenybopper makeup job turning her into some famous pop-tart yowler, which makes her frown. But she gets them to rim her eyes with kohl and dab on red lipstick, and she scores some cream foundation, which makes her look what they call "porcelain" and what I call "ghostly"—or ghastly. Lynwood insists she buy the blush in "Bridal Rose," although I know it is destined to go out in the circular file unless I catch it in time. Later on, I'm sure, June will hit Wacker's for the cheapo brand of eyeliner and other muck to add to the mix.

I decline to be "gussied up" (as the big-haired beauty consultant chomps out around her gum; if gum helps her think, then she's definitely wasting her gum.) June is today's star. Let her have her moment. The moment kind of scares me to death, but I can't look away from the evil transformation that will eventually take my sister away from me and add her to the community of sluts who disdain me and all nerd-geeks like me.

We float home in a curtain of that hideous perfume they spray over all customers who walk through the cosmetics department. Gary isn't home, which means the gods must be feeling merciful towards him.

"Wait until he gets back and sees how we look." Lynwood smiles beatifically.

Even though the only new paint I have on my face is cola-flavored LipLicker, I just roll my eyes. How can I know more about human nature than she does, at her age?

Men hate change in their women. Most guys hate short hair on chicks. They don't care much for all black, either, unless they're vampires. But anyhow, I know Gary can put on a good show when he senses the need.

Which he does. Like a good little soldier.

A few hours later, there's Mr. Bad Boyfriend again, parked out on the street in yet a different car. Looks like one of those square Kias, minus the hamsters. I call June over to her bedroom window for verification. At first she argues with me.

"It isn't him, Cru. Just looks a little like him."

"Exactly like him."

"I guess maybe around the eyes." She begrudges me the possibility for a moment. "Nose is similar. And the hair is the same, okay. But it isn't him. Lots of people look alike."

"It's him."

"So?" She expels a noise of exasperation and turns back to the mirror to study her lack of hair and pull at nonexistent strands. "Who cares?" This is a sure sign she's interested.

"Don't you get it? He's watching our house. To see if Arlene comes back."

Her eyes light up like cheap shards of broken glass in a kiln. "That's kind of rockin'. I'll go talk to him."

I'd been thinking more of siccing the cops on him.

But what I actually say is, "Should you really do that?"

"Don't talk to me. I don't like you." She adjusts her seductress skirt (one of Lynwood's impulse purchases last month, ignored until now), makes one last mirror check, and bangs out of the room.

Okay, I know I should watch from here with my cell phone in my hand, ready to call 911 when she gets abducted. But I never do the sensible thing in these situations.

She's doing the basic "hello sailor" routine when I pound up behind her. (I blame the mass media for teaching the homeschooled daughter of two progressives to default to thinking along such sexualized lines, but whatever.) "So what's your favorite band?" she purrs.

His lips curve upward in what I imagine he intends as a smile, but to me it looks like a viper getting ready to strike. "I'll listen to whatever. That's not what I came here to talk about."

"She shouldn't be talking to you at all," I insert, leaning around her.

She shoves me aside. "Cruelest, shut up and scrambola. This is a private conversation." My sister's glare would annihilate a lesser person.

"We're in a public place. And I'm on to his plan. Don't talk to him." I'm trying to pull my sister away, but we all know how well *that* ever works.

"What did she call you—Cruella?" He looks at me, bemused.

"Yas, and don't mess with me, dahlink, or I'll turn you into a coat," I say in a droll tone. It comes out more amusing than menacing, unfortunately.

"Ignore the child," says my sister, leaning into his car window as if she's going to plant a wet one on his forehead. "What was it you wanted to ask me?"

His lips make like curly brackets again. "Just trying to find out your connection. I mean, Arlene was here. I already know that. What did she come here for?"

"She's our cousin. We don't know where she's gone, but she keeps in touch." This is exactly the sort of thing June should not tell him.

"Yeah, I see the resemblance. Nice new hair, by the way." He actually reaches over and ruffles it as she simpers. This con artist sure knows how to sucker June in. "So does she come here often?"

"Now and then." June puts on a moony-cow face. "I'm sure she'll be back."

"Anything strange been happening since she left? Keeping any of her customers supplied while she's gone?"

I realize I've been chewing the life out of my cuticles and snatch my hands out of my mouth. Instead, I bite the inside of my cheek until it draws blood so I won't talk. He's staring at her hand, and the silver spoon starts to glow. It must be my imagination.

June fiddles with the ring, rotating it on her thumb, but that must be subconscious. As soon as she realizes what she's doing, she thrusts her hands behind her back. "No. She travels pretty light."

"Which way did she say she was headed?"

"Whichever way the wind blows." June tilts her head flirtatiously. "But she's not the only available female in the family."

With effort, I keep my eyes from rolling as the guy chuckles. "I'll keep that in mind. I might stop back by tonight."

"What time?"

I know he's after the ring. And the book. Arlene hid them with us so he, or whomever he represents, couldn't find them. He's trying to romance them out from under us. "June! You're not allowed to hang out with strange men."

"He doesn't look strange to me." She shoves me back, behind her.

I got nothing, so I punt. "She can't go. Our father is a big motorcycle gang member," I lie.

"I have a Hawg." He's looking at her hungrily. "Maybe you'd like to take a spin with me tonight."

"Our dad won't like that," I tell the guy. His eyes narrow, but he blinks to dismiss me as the bratty little sister. "She doesn't ride motorcycles."

"Cru. If the man wants me to ride…." She trails off, fluttering her lashes coquettishly.

He is eyeing the ring. Hungrily. It is not my imagination.

I look right at him. "I know what you want, and we're not telling." It pops out of my mouth without permission, before I know I'm going to say it, and I'm as surprised as they look.

This gained his attention for a moment. A half-smile plays around those snakes he uses for lips. Still, he makes no reply. He just turns that hungry gaze on me, running his dirty eyes up and down. Talk about creepy. I'm not going to let him intimidate me.

"She can't go anywhere with you," I tell him.

"I do what I want," she tells him.

"Sounds like a plan." He guns his engine. "See you later, then." She has just enough time to get her elbows off his window before he roars off into the ether.

As usual, I can't keep my mouth shut. "That might not have been such a cool idea."

"Shut up, Cru. You're an idiot." She tosses her head as if her hair could fly insouciantly around, having forgotten that it's gone. "You didn't manage to mess things up, for once. I'm going to meet him tonight."

"He didn't say what time. He only said he might." This brightens me up a bit, but she merely shrugs.

I suppose her sensors will be on full power all evening.

I wish I knew whether it would be better or worse to go tattle on her, and if I ought to do it now or later. Maybe I should follow them?

nightcrawler

Man, is June ever pissed.

It's nearly midnight and June has been staring out the window for hours. She spent the afternoon and early evening trying on everything in her closet plus some of the better stuff out of mine, putting together outfits, primping, and modeling for me and the mirror. She finally found something sufficiently trampy for a motor-cycle queen and started experimenting with shoes. She even went into Lynwood's closet to steal some stompy boots that haven't hit the pavement for several seasons, but they're black leather and nicely broken in. Lynwood would have two hissy fits if she knew, but she hasn't seen us since dinner. She's busy planning one of her Open House Tour Events for her real estate office. Gary is tied up with a big deal, so he has been on the phone most of the evening.

"He didn't say what time." I make my voice breezy. I don't want her to be hurt.

She doesn't say anything.

I decide to give her a little space.

Here's my thinking: this guy is probably going to show up, because I know he is after something, probably the book. He didn't take the ring when he had the chance today—but then again, it was playing dead. Or maybe he didn't want to snatch it in public in the daylight because he knew June would shriek and be heard by lots of people in the neighborhood. He wants to keep a low profile, especially from the police. Still, I have to wonder: Does the book know who he is, and that he's after it?

From my room, if I leave the bathroom door open (because it bridges our two rooms), I can see into June's room fairly well. I'll hear her rushing around when the guy drives up. In fact, I'll bet the entire city will hear her shriek of joy.

So I retrieve the mysterious book and settle on my bottom bunk. "Who are you?" I ask it, trying to strike a balance between a commanding question and a respectful inquiry. Opening it, at first I see a creamy white blank page. Empty.

But then a dot about the size of a freckle appears in the center of the page. The dot begins to move. It leaves behind a fine grey line. Like that old toy, the Etch-A-Sketch.

This time, I know for sure. There was nothing, and now there's something. It's drawing for me.

The lines multiply and it goes more quickly, like a Pictionary game on Adderall. An image of Arlene appears. She stands at a high window, her back to me, looking over a nighttime cityscape. Outside, the constellations appear to be flashing on and off.

The image becomes a video. It's like I'm watching YourTube on a tablet computer. The video zooms in on the night sky, where now the constellations aren't constellations, but groups of owls flying in formation.

What do you call a flock of owls? I'm sure there's a word. A "wisdom" or "an Athena," maybe.

Anyway, I can see them in the bright starlight of the city sky, swooping up and down, in and out among the canyons formed by the skyscrapers. It's mesmerizing. Is it in color, or black and white? You know, I can't really tell. When you're watching an old black-and-white movie, your mind fills things in. This video is like that.

This sequence fades out and an image of June fades in, lying on her bed sobbing. In color, this time, definitely. I get the clear feeling that she's hurting a lot worse than she'd be from some dumb date. The light from her bedroom window (in this new video scrolling by) glints off the silver ring like sparks. It also lets me see an owl in the tree outside her window (the one Gary calls her "window tree" and always quotes another Robert Frost poem about Fate and inner weather or some such nonsense). No, it's not just one owl—when the owl blinks, I notice a number of others perched in the branches around it, all blinking and swiveling their heads. Their eyes look like lasers, and their beams are trained on my sister.

Suddenly the book wrenches itself out of my trembling hands and slams itself. I am not imagining this.

All my clawing at the cover fails to reopen the book. Show's over.

My heart is pounding. I could use a puff off of June's old asthma inhaler (she doesn't need them any more, but I feel as if the air has been sucked out of my room.) There's even a sheen of sweat on my palms.

But at least I have gotten another bash from the clue-stick. I know for sure now that June's unexpected transformation is not merely a rush of hormones. And my intuition screams that I'm somehow about to be drawn into this book's mission. Because this book has something it wants done, and it intends to use me to do it.

That sends an icy serpent down my backbone. I realize I'm freezing, despite the expensive climate control system in this house. As a control freak, I really don't like the idea of being used. Especially by something that I don't yet understand.

Sorcery…compulsion…anyone? Bueller? Anyone?

I stash the book back into its hidey-hole and retreat to my bunk to puzzle it all out.

"He stood me up."

My line of sight through the bathroom mirror into June's dim room isn't good, but her lower lip, usually stiff or pouty, might be trembling. Is that a tear in the corner of her Cleopatra eye?

She slides off her vanity stool and starts pacing. "That jerk. I'll show him."

Am I a bad person for feeling relieved—even happy?

It's obvious, apparent, undeniable that the guy was simply yanking June's chain. I can't imagine why, except he's a typical male. I really thought he'd show up, but maybe something derailed his little-engine-that-could.

Anyway, she takes a while to deflate. She finally sheds her finery, hangs everything up, and sits in her undies at the vanity. It used to be a desk but now can only be called a vanity, as all books are banished and it is arrayed with June's collection of tramp-paint. She smears cold cream on her face and brushes the glitter out of her hair to some extent, then bolts herself into the bathroom to "wash up." Or maybe to have a good cry.

I'm exhausted. Time for the peace and quiet of my iPod tuned to the Schubert Ländler playlist and that novel I started the other night. I only get through a couple of pages before I feel myself nodding off.

I wake up in the dark gasping for air.

A hand is clamped over my nose and mouth, and something heavy has my whole body pinned against the mattress so forcefully I can feel every pea.

"Keep still and I won't hurt you," says the Dark One. "You know what I want, and that's all I want." A cold breeze flutters my curtains and I notice the window is propped wide. Lynwood was right about not leaving the window cracked open at night, after all.

He's got my wrists pinned against the pillow above my head with his free hand and starts tugging on my fingers. "Where is it? You had it on earlier. You'd better not try to pull anything."

I can't even cough. He's so stupid that he's come into the wrong room. "Mmmph" is all I can manage.

Everything's going black. His hand stinks like a stepped-in cow patty. Can I kick my bedpost hard enough that the footboard falls off and brings Gary running the way it did back when I was having nightmares last year? I swing my foot, but a heavy boot scrapes down my shinbone to stop me and it hurts. A lot.

A retching noise starts in my throat. He'd better move that hand. When I do the rainbow yawn, it pulses out hard like it has to be at work on time. I can't control it.

Is his grip loosening just a tad? Surely he knows what this sound presages.

Another awful urpy sound echoes under his palm. He lets up a bit on the pressure, as if he's still not quite sure what he's dealing with.

I have to be sitting up so I don't choke on my own vomit, just in case I do barf, and it's fifty-fifty right now. Adrenaline grants me superhuman strength as I struggle to sit up. It's like in a bad horror flick where a demon is about to pop out of the girl, and I'm the lucky girl.

I manage to push him partially aside as more noises ensue. Looking uncertain, he lets the stink-hand slip down to my chin. Bad choice. He rears back just as I projectile-hurl my dinner all over his face. Broccoli stinks just as much coming up as it does going down. Also, when I barf, it's pretty loud. It always is.

June is super sensitive to noises. The bathroom light flicks into life and she bangs into the doorway. "Cruelest, you know I hate that SOUND. Can't you remember to — " She stops short.

He glances back and forth between us a couple of times. Backlighted in the bathroom glare, she's obviously the one he intended to "persuade."

Their gazes lock. He tosses me off the bed and leaps for her, knocking her to the bathroom's tile floor.

I hear someone screaming. It's me.

Shouting what sounds like "I call upon Asmodeus Mogart" (surely not "Amadeus Mozart," who sides with the angels), the devil-boy grapples with my sister. Formidable as she is, he's still a lot bigger. He wrestles her flat and traps her wrists between his meaty hands. She fights back, kicking and shouting obscenities.

He's got her hand and is pulling mightily on the ring. He doesn't care if he tears her finger off, as far as I can tell. He opens his mouth and tries to maneuver her flicking finger inside, as if to bite.

But this blackguard has not counted on our parents. Gary bursts in, followed by Lynwood in her filmy nightgown. When Gary sees what's happening, he leaps across the room, grabs the intruder by the back of the neck, and drags him off of June. He backs into my bedroom and puts the guy into a half-nelson. Maybe even a full Nelson.

Gary roars, "By God, I'll kill you!" The guy starts gasping for breath.

Obviously, Gary thinks the guy was "just" raping her. He couldn't know what the guy is really after. It's probably just as well. There's no rational way I can warn him that magic is afoot.

June's crying now and gasping, hugging her hands to her chest. Our brave daddy (and I feel a great surge of love and admiration for him right now) is beating the slimeball's head against the floor, but what with my thick pink carpet and white Flokati area rug atop it, he probably isn't doing enough damage.

Lynwood, using my antique pink Princess phone, already has 911 on the line.

All of a sudden Gary cries out and releases the Dark One's head. He clutches at his own abdomen. I didn't see him get hit, but maybe the guy somehow kicked his solar plexus. At the same time, I notice the blackguard is glimmering. Not shimmering, exactly…it's more like he's fading out.

Gary's face starts turning purple and both Lynwood and June rush to grab him as he collapses backwards. June trips on the edge of my Flokati and goes down. Gary flails backwards into Lynwood like he's been sucker-punched, and they topple in a tangle of arms and legs onto the rug next to June.

That's why no one but me sees the evil one glow-and-flow into a new state of matter (no, seriously—cold plasma? Protoplasm, as the spiritualists would have called it?) He pulsates a moment and then congeals into the form of a large black bird. The crow (raven? I have no idea; it's the size of a small hawk) spreads its wings and flaps into the air, heading out the window into the open night sky.

Gary doesn't look seriously hurt, to me; he's merely been clocked (not that it isn't a bad thing). Perhaps I'm in denial, though, because my mother and sister are hysterical and panicky.

Lynwood is getting into position to breathe into Gary's mouth (possibly following the instructions the 911 dispatcher is giving her) when he starts coughing. "He's definitely breathing," Lynwood says into the phone. "The burglar made him pass out, but he's conscious now. He's blinking."

I can't tell her that I think it was a magical knockout. I'm just thankful that the spell wasn't any more powerful.

June is now in hysterics on the floor and Lynwood is busy telling the 911 voice to send ambulances and police and the SWAT team and the National Guard for all I know. Black helicopters will probably arrive momentarily.

In response to something they say to her on the phone, Lynwood glances around, then turns to me because I'm the only one who seems coherent ("seems" being the operative term). "Where did he go?"

I'm still considering how to say this without being sent to the loony bin for observation when June chokes out, "He jumped out the window." She rushes to poke her head through the opening, apparently hoping to see him splattered on the lawn. "There's no ladder leaning against the wall. Too dark to see where he went."

"The intruder's outside the house now," Lynwood is telling the phone when Gary rears up, shakes his head as though to clear it, and tries to stand. "No, babe, stay still," she admonishes him.

"What happened?" Gary doesn't remember the encounter at all. He thinks he came in here to check on us and just fainted.

We give statements to the responding officers. Gary refuses to be taken to the hospital, insisting to the EMTs that he is fine, although I can see a bruise on his chest when they're checking him over and the paramedics insist on giving him some oxygen. June lets a cute tech give her oxygen (I suspect because she wants to know how it feels, having read the James Bond novel that has 007 getting giddy on an overdose of oxygen), but she isn't really hurt and Lynwood assures the paramedics she'll bring June to the emergency room if she lets out even a peep. No one is going to be able to sleep tonight.

I don't want to be fussed over, so I don't mention that the guy touched me. I'm all right. Yes, I am bruised, and my lip feels like it's inflated to 200 PSI. Tomorrow I'll be aching and sore. That boot-heel he scraped down from my knee to my ankle broke the skin, and it throbs, but it isn't bloody or scabbed or whatever.

Still, I don't feel safe in my room, so I'm going to sleep on June's floor in a pallet made out of her old comforter and a couple of quilts that Lynwood keeps for guests. I smell Lynwood's Musky Jasmine Flowers perfume on the pillow, but it doesn't comfort me.

The lights are on all through the house, perhaps because the EMTs came upstairs and they needed to see, but Lynwood and Gary have made no move to turn them off. Except in here, where we have only the bedroom lamps on the lowest setting. No one is complaining they can't sleep in all this light, either.

Our parents' bedroom door is closed but I can hear every word of their argument, which has been raging since the cops left us with advice to get an alarm system and TURN IT ON EVERY NIGHT. Our enclave has been pretty safe, which explains why Gary decided to stop paying for the old BrinkOfDoom system that we had. But he'll be getting a new high-tech one plus a moat with sharks and velociraptors tomorrow at dawn.

"I can't believe this could happen," Lynwood keeps saying.

"It's that hair and those clothes." Gary is really off his launch pad and well into the ionosphere. "Overnight, you let her turn into a tramp, and now look what happens."

"It's not *her* fault if some man behaves like a brute," Lynwood begins.

I tune it out. They're roving over well-trodden ground, and if they need to argue until they're both worn-out enough to sleep, well, so be it.

June turns over, noisily. She coughs. "Cruelest?"

I don't answer right away.

She sits up. "Cru? Are you OK?"

"I guess." I discover I'm hoarse. We never did tell them the whole story, just that this guy was hanging around earlier, and they remembered him from before as the joyride dude. They don't know he went for me first. They don't need to worry even more.

I shift in my cocoon and turn my back to June.

"You sure?"

I mumble something. She's not getting off easy this time.

Finally she says something that I consider necessary before we open any channels of serious communication. "I'm sorry."

"Not your fault," I say, because protocol dictates that's the nice thing to say, although I do feel it kind of was her fault, duh.

"It sort of is. My, um, fault."

She never goes that far in admitting responsibility. I roll over and look at her. "Now do you believe me? Something freaky's going on, and Arlene is into it deep."

"Well." She blinks. "I suppose all evidence points to that."

"There's something about that ring." I twist around and sit up to examine her swollen finger. "You never take it off because it won't come off any more, will it?"

"Shut up," she whispers. "I could get it off if I really wanted to."

I don't argue. "The ring is a link. Back to Arlene, I mean. She's in touch with you along some magical line of force."

"I know," she whispers. She doesn't elaborate.

"The book, too." I'm about to core-dump the secrets of the tome when June sits up again and takes a rude tone of voice with me.

"What book? You're not talking about that diary thing you keep dragging around, the one with your dumb 'what I did today' and reviews of the idiot books you're reading and so forth?" She crumples her pillow under her head. "I've seen that. It doesn't have anything to do with Arlene."

"That's where you're wrong. It's actually a magic book. Arlene hid it behind your dresser drawer. That's what I was getting when you caught me and Gary in your room."

She snorts. "I saw that book, and so did he. It was only that old Bible. You can't shit me."

"No, it's magic. It just makes people think it is something else."

This time her noise of exasperation says she thinks the events of the evening have been too much for me, and she's at the end of her own "merrie rope," as well. She turns over and pounds her pillow. She's going to turn the stuffing into lumps, doing that.

"I'm not kidding."

"Oh, go to sleep."

arlene's a peel

I can't sleep. With some maneuvering, I manage to crawl out of the tangled cocoon on June's bedroom floor without waking her. It's tough, but I make myself be brave and go into my bedroom. Shadows swirl and the moonlight plays across my tainted bedcovers. I'm quivering like the school cafeteria's gelatin special. But I need to ask someone (or *something*) a question.

Talk about your feet being frozen to the floor. I'm a real chicken, but finally I bolt over to my hiding place and yank out the book. This is all its fault, or its owner's, anyway. So it can damn well tell me what's going on. It knows. I am sure of that.

Gingerly I crack the cover and peer inside the book to see what, if anything, it might like to say to me. "Give me a hint," I tell it, knocking lightly on the front leather. Maybe it doesn't speak English. I try French, Spanish, German, and Esperanto.

Nothing. I see only a blank grid-lined notebook, ready to serve as a lab journal for any twisted mad scientists who might come along. I slam it as a kind of punishment and shove it under my pillow. Let it wallow in the evil miasma of bad vibes and see how it likes that. Maybe later it'll feel like talking to me in exchange for a nicer hidey-hole.

I crawl back to June's floor and somehow doze off. I think I remember dreaming of angels.

At breakfast everyone acts fairly subdued, which is unusual for our household. They don't even notice how little I can force down. Or how much June manages to pack away. I'm not hungry, but June eats everything I slip onto her plate when they're not looking, so Lynwood beams at me when she picks up my shiny dish.

Lynwood and Gary are completely occupied watching the workmen install the alarm system. Lynwood shrieked into the phone at dawn and told the answering service at Safety Is Our Business that she needed An Emergency Installation. The owner of the company was out here at eight o'clock sharp going over our floor plan with them and showing them the Premium/Executive Level of Security. I don't know how much extra they're paying to get it done today, ASAP. But it makes me feel guilty. After all, I opened that window.

June is too quiet as she disappears from the table. I find her curled into the window seat on our stair landing, flipping through a magazine she bought at the convenience store. *InkWorld.*

"Why would you waste"—I check the price—"six dollars on that?" It looks simply gross.

"Thinking of taking on ink."

"You what?"

"Getting a tattoo, you idiot."

"Like Arlene's barbed wire bracelets with the hearts that are speared on the barbs and bleeding? Eeuww."

She cuts her gaze at me from under hooded eyelids. I am beneath contempt. To underscore this, she rolls out of the window seat and flounces downstairs.

I'm halfway to my own room when my heart starts beating like a tom-tom.

Ridiculous. Last night I went in, and I didn't turn to Jell-O. No reason to wig out this morning. Still, I stop in the doorway and take a few deep breaths. I can't let the intrusion besmirch (another SAT word) my personal turf.

With the sunlight beaming in through my sheer flowered curtains, everything looks back to normal. I step tentatively inside. This is my space, and I claim it again, without a smudging or an exorcism, just by jumping onto my bare mattress. (Lynwood stripped the bed-clothes, and the maids will replace them when they get here later today. At least I think this is their day.) It doesn't take long for my palpitations to quiet down and my teeth to stop chattering. It's daytime, and the guy is long gone. As the song says, everything's all right. (Not "alright." Alright is alwrong, says Miss Grammar.)

I should try to do some schoolwork. June and I turn in our exams and papers by e-mail to this online Mind-spell Academy where we're enrolled to satisfy the state, except for the daily stuff that Lynwood is supposed to grade (and sometimes she even does grade it.) We have to do these online quizzes and Web page worksheets every few days or Lynwood starts getting e-mails from the proprietors about our slacking off. I know June hasn't done a lick of coursework in over a week.

My laptop needs charging, so I plug it in and surf over to do the SAT Question of the Day.

A word problem, and it's really simple. I see the three prime factors of the given number right off, and use that to plug in the values they want. $47369 = 7 \times 67 \times 101$. Too easy.

People often jump to the conclusion that we home-school for religious reasons. (Gary often says his reli-gion is worship of the Almighty Dollar. Lynwood is far more ecumenical.) Actually we're autodidacts, meaning we pretty much teach ourselves what we'd otherwise have had dragged out over a far longer time. It started when June was six and kept coming home from first grade crying because the kids teased her. She's supposedly some sort of genius, my sister, according to the re-sults of some test or another. She's bright, I'll grant you. But I think I'm smarter than she is. I just don't test well. On purpose.

The paperwork for the school district has me down as "gifted" with an "elevated, extensive (translate: show-offy) vocabulary." I also have good intuition, which is even more useful. It's better that people don't know what I'm thinking, because I'm always thinking, and most people don't like that. Besides, after seeing the hoo-hah everyone made over June's test scores, I re-solved to answer at least half the questions wrong on those kinds of tests. It worked, because now when I can do things, they applaud and cheer. If they knew how I can do math in my head (I don't really "DO" any-thing: when I see an equation or read a math prob-lem, the solution simply plays itself out in my head like I'm watching a mental computer screen), it would be a real problem. Nobody but June knows; they'd have me in college or something, and I do not want to be their Sheldon Cooper wannabe.

After filling in a few pages of each subject online (and choosing three vocabulary words to use in sentences today: "magistrate," "nonplussed," and "dingleberry" — okay, I just threw that last one in for laughs), I trek down to the kitchen for a diet cola. Lynwood and Gary are standing at the counter elbow-to-elbow poring over the security company's blueprint. They exchange Meaning-ful Looks over my head and I smile weakly, as they are expecting me to do.

Gary tousles my hair—which hasn't adjusted to the new weed-whacker style and is sticking up in back like some New Wave mistake—and mumbles, "Take it easy today, hon."

Lynwood says in that fake-bright voice, "Why don't you read one of your new books?" I've already read them all.

"I'll be online. We have a lot of schoolwork." They look so happy and relieved, possibly because I can vocalize at all after my Traumatic Experience (they don't know the half of it.)

"Make sure you get me that book report." Gary's forced grin betrays his hidden stress.

"Oh, definitely." It takes a second to remember what he's talking about. That Robin Hood disguise Arlene's trickster of a book pulled on him (it's more of a grimoire; another SAT word, but that's a more appropriate term).

That reminds me. First order of business is for me to check the grimoire and see what it might have changed into today. Maybe it's having an identity crisis, like my sister.

This time, Esperanto works. The front page comes to life like an LCD screen, swirling with colors. Writing flows across the page in Arlene's antique penmanship.

But I don't like what it's scribbling before my eyes. "HELP!"

A blue dot appears below the word. It starts moving, leaving behind a drawing like an Etch-A-Sketch does. It's Arlene, tied hand and foot to a four-poster with the

Dark One standing over her with a sword. Under the sketch, more words appear in that "bleeding" font that looks like quill pen and ink that hasn't dried. "SAVE ME, APRIL."

My heart speeds up and then pounds in my ears. I feel faint. How can I answer her? This isn't exactly a BlackBerry and I can't just text her back. I'm not a witch or a sorceress or a magician or even any good at card tricks. What am I supposed to do?

Like any good nerd, I panic. This is not the type of thing I can take to Lynwood or Gary or the cops. I would end up on the analyst's couch, heavily medicated, while Arlene gets sacrificed. Besides, what would the book show them? I don't want to find out.

June is my only hope, unless I find a red phone that speaks directly to God. And I'm pretty sure only Popes and Pomeranians speak directly to God.

"You'd better cooperate with me this time," I instruct the grimoire. "Don't erase that. We need June's help. Persuade her." Tucking the book into my waistband, I head out to the treehouse, where (as I predicted) June is immersed in her magazine.

She watches me climb the ropes, impassive. Turning away, she barks, "Get out of here. Leave me alone."

The book is already open to the scary drawing. Gaining purchase on the floorboards, I thrust the page between my sister and her tattered periodical. "You need to see this. I mean, see it as it really is."

"What?" She glances up. "Last year's math book. You breezed through that. You don't need my help."

"It's not a math book. It's Arlene's book." I try to show it to her again.

She shoves me away. "Go live with your books some-where else. I'm joining the real world." Her eyes and her ring flash as she pushes back what's left of her hair.

I have to make June see before she is lost to me for-ever.

"LOOK at the page, just for a minute. Pretend you're me and see through my eyes. Use your astral vision, like you said when we were doing the Tarot cards last month."

"That's kid stuff. I'm not going to play that any more." She sounds irritated, flipping through samples of various multicolored tattoos. One particularly gross abdominal tat shows an open wound with some kind of messed-up innards below. Why would people do that?

I slam the book on top of the gross pages again. "You have to see this. At least try. It's a matter of life or death, Arlene says."

"Arlene?" She narrows her eyes at me. "She called?"

"No! She's trying to communicate with us. Through the book."

My sister stands up and gets ready to toss me out of the treehouse. She has me by the armpits and is swinging me towards the "exit" before I can get another word out. June is a Scorpio, the sign of sex and death and other peo-ple's money—and the scorpion has a nasty stinger that it doesn't hesitate to plunge into your soft spots.

"I know you're skeptical," I gasp, despite the stress. "Scorpios are very skeptical. But if you'll just let me show you, I can prove it." I wince, playing the sympathy card. "I'm still sore from last night."

"You're gonna think sore when you land on your butt in the turf." But she's relenting, obviously thinking of my ordeal with the Dark One. She has already pulled my right shoulder joint from the first position to the second, which kind of hurts when someone other than me does it, although I'm sure she doesn't realize.

I hang from her hands for another moment, and then I land on the floor. Is she having a cramp, or just a moment of compassion? Second thoughts about my claims?

It's pain, because she's clasping her hands. No, she's doing something with that ring, twirling it and moving it up and down. "Frack it, the sparks hurt," she murmurs cryptically.

I wait for further elucidation. Instead, she shows a bit of curiosity. "What did you say about the book?" She hands it back to me from where it had plopped at our feet when she snatched me up.

Quickly I explain again about finding the grimoire and not being able to get anybody to see it for what it is. My fingers and toes are all crossed for luck. "Just give me a chance to convince you."

She tilts her head and sits. "Cruelest, you are an idiot and an airhead and a geek, but for some reason I don't think you would carry a stupid joke this far. I'll give you"—she glances at her new designer watch, a Mickey Rat—"three minutes. Then you're going down the rope."

"That sounds fair." I steady the book on her lotus-position knees. It's still showing me the awful drawing, but I don't know what it's letting her see. "Concentrate."

She drops her eyelids to half-mast, and I realize I have to give more instruction than that. I'm desperate, punting again. Wait: maybe it's like those "3-D" images of sailboats that were so popular when we were kids. Although I could see them, and she never could. "Cross your eyes and look just *beyond* the plane of the page, like with Magic Eye."

To her credit, she squints and stares. She gasps. "I think I see writing. I see something."

But she isn't looking on the proper page. She's gaping at the next page, a blood-red page where words are appearing in the old Macintosh "ransom note" font.

PLEASE JUNIE MOONY HELP ME—It HURTS SO BAD

The same sketch re-draws itself with a speedy glowing line, grosser this time. Now a bloodied Arlene is being threatened with a Morningstar, which is not a heavenly body but one of those medieval torture weapons.

My sister grabs my perma-bruise and applies pressure. "Is this a trick? I don't find this stuff amusing."

"It's not a joke. It's real." I stare into her eyes. "The book didn't trust anyone but me before, but it's talking to you now. It's confiding in you because it knows I need your help to help Arlene. Please, June. For once, *believe*."

She's thinking. I can see it. June has read all the Harry Potter books and the Narnia books, and she used to love fairy tales. "I swear to you by...." One of the problems of being a rationalist is that you have nothing to swear by. "On my Mensa membership card."

The book starts to shake violently, and we both instinctively grasp it. It immediately shows Arlene tied to a stretcher and being carried into a dark forest.

June looks at me, then back at the book.

"Dammit, tell me where she is," she shouts at the page. "I need a location, a map, an address." When nothing of the sort materializes, she gets angrier. "What a useless retard."

The page deigns to go blank upon the latter insult, and I figure it's within its rights. June tends to turn rude and out of control when she doesn't get her way.

I tear it loose from her grip. "This is NOT the way. You're obviously violating the protocol for communing with a magical item. You sent it into a sulk. Let me." I stroke its binding and coo to it for a moment as June fumes and makes faces. "Come on, she's just ignorant and she's upset and worried about our cousin. Give us a break and let me talk to...to whoever you are."

After a good long pause (if it was intending to put a scare into me, it worked), it glows out some letters. All uppercase, so that I know it means business.

YOU MUST BE RESPECTFUL
WHEN YOU ADDRESS THE
HIDDEN POWERS

"Excuse me," June mumbles sullenly.

I phrase it humbly: "We are ever so regretful that we forgot ourselves, O Powers."

June follows my lead in a more respectful tone of voice. "What do you ask of us, O Powers, in order that we might save the lovely Arlene?"

The page answers in mega-flourished script.

Ask not specifics until you have complied with the orders. The powers are at their leisure. They have all the time in the world, and you must come before them as one who is properly initiated into their ways

OMG. We absolutely cannot become witches. Lynwood would have a cross-eyed fit.

"What orders?" June slams her fist into her other palm. "Why does it talk so oddly instead of just coming out and telling us what it wants?"

Even though she addressed it indirectly, it is kind enough to answer. Enigmatically, of course.

All priests speak thusly so as to conceal secrets from the uninitiated but to reveal them to the adept

"So how do I become an adept?"

The page goes blank.

I sigh exaggeratedly to make her pay attention. "It knows—they know—you're not serious. You don't want to become an adept. You're just trying to snow it to jump this hurdle." I let some smugness creep into my tone as I lord it over June, being the one the pages prefer to talk to.

"Well, I'm going online to look it up." She starts pounding madly on her laptop, which she keeps out here and which is somehow always charged. "Witchcraft, the occult, initiation," she mutters, emitting search terms under her breath.

My sister can find anything on the net. If she can't find it, it's not worth knowing. I await enlightenment from her, as the book seems to be quiescent (you guessed it, another SAT jewel).

I'm about to close the book when the page wipes itself blank and new shimmering, spidery letters speak to me.

Look through the spyglass to the north

As casually as possible, trying not to attract June's attention so she won't snatch it away, I take the eyepiece and scan the street. Nothing much is happening. Slowly I pan across in the direction I think is true north, towards the greenspace. At the edge of the woods, I sense movement.

It's a person. A man. Twisting the focus rings this way and that, I try to make sure of what I'm seeing. I can't help gasping.

Naturally, my sister leaps up and pulls the eyepiece away. "What?" She swivels the scope to see. "That creep."

She looks pissed as she flips open her cell phone. "Hello? I'd like to report a peeper. Yes, ma'am, he was looking in our window a moment ago, and he's the same one who was in the yellow Hummer and got sent away yesterday by the officers on patrol. Now he's at the edge of the woods behind our house, lurking. It frightens me. Yes, thank you so much. No, my parents are here, I'm all right. Just wanted to report this." She gives our catty-corner neighbors' address and a fake name ("Trula Pureheart") and snaps the phone shut. "Get your stuff."

"Why? The police'll be here in a minute, and they'll chase him away."

"That's not the point. I mean, sure, he's roasted, toasted, and crispy. But we need to know where he is going. He's going to lead us to Arlene. I'm sure of it. Or at least to the clues we need."

"How?" I'm afraid that I already know how, and I can't think of a way to deflect this.

June already has her laptop stowed in her backpack, and now she pokes her arms through the straps. "We're going to follow him." She hefts herself off the platform and swings down the rope like Jane of the Jungle.

"But that's dangerous." I scramble to catch up.

"Hurry up, Cruelest. We may not have much time."

a cantrip a day

*"I **don't think** this* is a good idea," is what I would normally say, but I swallow it when I see June's glittering eyes. She's really hauling butt.

I manage to get the grimoire tucked behind the front of my denim jacket so I can get down the rope ladder using both hands. I always feel as if I'm going to get tangled up in the ropes, and June would let me hang there by my shoelaces while she laughed. But the ladder seems to know this is important and doesn't trip me.

When I catch up with my sister, she's still muttering. "It's payback time." She looks grim. "The cops won't do a thing but hassle him. Until he actually kills somebody, they can't do anything about stalking. But by Athena's leap out of Zeus's head, I swear I will."

That's a new oath for her. I can't help but wonder where she picked it up.

We have to get past our parents. Gary is watching intently, arms crossed tightly over his starched striped button-down, as the security company's crew hooks up the various alarm panels all around the house. He's fascinated by work—claims he can watch it for hours, it's terribly relaxing—and he always says he can learn something from studying a great craftsperson at labor. Lynwood is bending the ear of the foreman on the job about just where to attach the "breakage panel detectors" on each and every window and French door windowpane so they won't mess up the décor, but will still vibrate with the slightest touch of a sledgehammer. They won't miss us for hours, if ever.

I do not think this is a good idea and I don't want to go. They say June is a genius, but I can't forget how I read somewhere that part of genius is the supreme capacity for getting its possessor into trouble of all kinds. I have to admit that sometimes the dead white European males had a point or were even right.

But I can't let her go by herself. So I slip inside to grab my backpack (prepacked for Lynwood's frequent impulse road trips and other emergencies) off my side chair. At the door of my room, I hesitate. Most of my important possessions are already in this—including my iPod, digital camera, tablet computer (lighter than a clunky laptop and with an AirCard so I can get online without WiFi), mini sewing kit, a couple of favorite books, and so forth. My laptop isn't that heavy when added to the mix.

I have this funny feeling we're going to be gone over-night, or at least for a while. It's easy enough to roll a couple of changes of underwear, two pairs of socks, a pair of black leggings, and two tank tops and fit them in around my stuff. I can wear double tops under my denim jacket and then un-layer if I get overheated. Although I'm always cold.

At the last minute I tuck in one of my personal talis-mans. It's the New Testament that Nana gave me when I visited her church with her. It's palm-sized and came from a Billy Graham Crusade that she went to years ago. She wrote my name in it with a real fountain pen from the 1950s, a Parker pen, in peacock blue ink that has faded a bit. Talismans can be good or bad. I definitely need something to counterbalance that wicked book of Arlene's.

Speaking of which, I'm going to hide it in my back-pack's inner zipper pocket in the back where you are supposed to keep your math homework and other pa-pers that shouldn't be creased. Who'd look for anything important there, in some schoolgirl's backpack?

It's unlikely that someone would steal anything that looks like a textbook these days. No one cares about studying any more. The world has become a cesspool of imbeciles, and a full cesspool of imbeciles is apparently more important to preserve than an eyedropper of bril-liance.

I'm good to go.

But first, I flip the grimoire open just to see if it might have any advice. After all, it must have known (if there is a consciousness behind this, and for now it's easiest for me to think of it as having one) that we'd take off running to rescue Arlene. That's what it wants. Isn't it?

Immediately it starts texting to me in spidery fountain-pen handwriting. It's kind of like reading that reproduction Declaration of Independence that Gary has framed behind his desk.

You must not be seen

I blink. "When we're following the Dark One?" I don't know his name, but I've been thinking of him as "Asmodeus" ever since that little scene in the bedroom. I suppose the book will know who I mean. "Um. How are we going to stay hidden?"

Cast the Cantrip of

Unnoticeability

Sure, a cantrip, right: a folk-magic spell straight out of Dungeons and Dragons. Is it kidding me? Probably not; it never kids (so far).

"I don't know it." I wait.

After a moment the page displays the charm in a more readable font. It's written as a sort of sonnet, although it hardly scans like Shakespeare's (iambic pentameter being tough even for sorcerous artifacts, it appears).

"Unnoticeability." Okay. I can see this being awfully useful, actually. I suppose I asked, so I should pay heed.

Following its instructions carefully, I place my hands on either side of my face and poof my cheeks out like a chipmunk. Then I let the air slowly out as I say the charm.

> *"The light that shines upon my face*
> *Now from his ken we must erase.*
> *Hide as well my sister, too,*
> *As she has her own work to do.*
> *If we want others to see (we won't).*
> *They will—but we don't.*
> *Unnoticeable shall we two be*
> *For days of three, so mote it be."*

Nothing happens. Except there's a funny cramp in my right shoulder. I work it around between the two positions of my "double" joint without even thinking. Then I notice the page displaying a question. A math question to trigger a spell?

But I do know the answer immediately.

"The greatest common factor of 1344 and 1856 is 64," I say aloud.

A spray of ethereal sparks hits me all over, all at once. It's gentle on my skin, making me crackle like when you get shocked by static electricity by touching something metal in the winter, but soft like grains of talcum powder instead. The scent of gardenias wafts past. The sixty-four unique factors of 7560 (two cubed, times three cubed, times five, times seven) occur to me in a rainbow swipe. Far away, snatches of a somehow familiar tune tease at my mind's ear, then fade. And my shoulder snaps back into the main joint, feeling fine.

What else could these freaky things mean other than the cantrip has worked?

The writing disappears. Again I am staring at a blank page. As I continue looking, it becomes an orange mandala that begins to spin slowly.

Time to close the book before it hypnotizes me or something. I don't intend to be a Manchurian Candidate or a zombie doing its bidding. I'm only into this magic stuff until we get Arlene safely home. It's way too dangerous—and enticing.

I hope I've done things properly. You can't exactly call tech support for one of these things.

By the time I'm downstairs, June has her laptop case hitched up like a get-along across her torso and is stashing a couple of water bottles and some miscellaneous gear in its many pockets. She keeps a lot of cool stuff in there. I wonder whether she even has one change of underwear.

Spotting me, she straddles her bike. "Come on!"

We ride. Near the entrance to our development we see the flashing lights and the cop talking to the idiot, as predicted. We dally by the creek's waterfall bridge. The perp looks around, and I hear June chanting something under her breath. A poem. My intuition tells me it is actually an incantation. A spell.

She's been looking up this stuff on the net, just as I knew she would. When June buys into something, she empties the savings account. If this is for real, the guy may turn into a toad. Any minute now. I hold my breath.

But even as she speaks, I can feel the spell bouncing or cracking or fumbling, whatever they call it. She stomps the ground gently three times with each foot, like a counting horse. Her ring flashes, but dulls again to a tarnished glow.

It didn't work.

How do I know? It's just a feeling. But the cantrip that the book had me do charged the air and all but rang an ethereal bell overhead so that I knew power had gone out from me—rather, from the book, I suppose. All I feel from this is a cosmic "thud."

But she thinks it has worked, and grins back at me. "Now all I need is a material sacrifice."

Involuntarily I shift away. I don't want her to get any ideas.

She pulls something out of her pocket. It looks like a pigeon feather or maybe just a piece of grey felt. Shredding it, she sprinkles it on the ground beneath her feet, then grinds it in with a final word of power that sounds like "gronk" but can't possibly be in any language I know. And I have snippets of Esperanto, German, French, Latin, and Navajo.

Still nothing. No power has been drawn from the Ineffable Springs. My sister is a poser and a dabbler, so I'm not surprised that whatever she found on the net didn't work; she's not committed and hasn't attached her will and intention to the cause. Everyone knows that's what it takes to succeed at something like this. But she seems happy, so I play along.

Our perp is not looking at us, but what with all this activity (she's being ultra quiet—for June, I mean—but it's not like we're hiding), I'm still nervous that he'll spot us. My cantrip was Unnoticeable, not Invisible. Although we plan to pursue him, I wouldn't want the tables to turn and get us chased.

Falling silent, June paws through her all-purpose portable hole and pulls out a couple of red paisley bandanas. She rubs them lightly on the ground she's just stomped and then folds them into huge triangles, the dirtied sides to the inside. Handing me one, she half-smiles. "Put this on as a headwrap," she commands quietly. "And get your sunglasses."

Good idea. I slap the bandana over my too-identifiable hair; it does a great job of making me look different, really it does. All my hair fits under it. I look practically bald, which may or may not make me stand out less. Still, I pull out my sunglasses, because the Texas sun can only enhance the pounding headache I'm bound to get. June wears the classic Ray-Ban Club Master style in black. She always says they make her feel like a 60's politician crossed with Malcolm X. Mine are more in the vein of Four-Eyed Pride: huge squarish lozenges, some kind of weird tortoiseshell plastic frames.

My sister fancies herself a master of disguise, but I suspect we look like a couple of B-52s rejects.

"Unnoticeable" may not be enough. But it'll have to do.

Anyway, they don't spy us. As soon as the officer backs away, the jackass takes off on foot across the woods.

It's easy enough to ride on the paved bike path and follow.

The path winds along the Old Katy Trail (named after the railroad, paved for the yuppies to jog on.) I figure he'll stop in the next greenspace to regroup, but he doesn't. He keeps going all the way to the DART train station.

Hey, I can handle this. I love our light rail.

We lock our bikes onto the rack and I get tickets from the machine (I have the change from my emergency twenty and I know June has money because she always does) and wait at the other end of the platform. He is smoking and looks like he'd have smoke coming out of his ears if not for his cigs to relieve the stress.

The DART train is waiting. He steps on, and we wait for the warning horn to enter at the last moment. We're two cars down from him, but I can see the stupid red beanie cap he's wearing and I'll know if he gets off. Nope, he rides all the way downtown to Dallas' Union Station.

From here I have a fine view of the Dallas Morning News building. Engraved on the building's front is the

motto, *"Build the news upon the rock of truth and righteous-
ness; conduct it always upon the lines of fairness and integrity;
acknowledge the right of the people to get from the newspaper both sides of every important question."* I'm musing on
the possibilities of becoming a journalist and writing a
travel article about all this when we spy our prey survey-
ing the area. We hunker down, but he doesn't appear to
notice us.

We lurk on the platform reading the historical mark-
ers until he wanders inside the Amtrak station. June
rummages through her pack and retrieves that Hear-
ing-Ear spy thing she ordered off TV. I fear she's attract-
ing too much attention as she scans the crowd for him
(people ARE looking at us, and I cringe a lot.) Suddenly
she grips my arm in a tourniquet with both hands. I see
what she's excited about: he came out another door and
is getting on the platform to take the next train. He's
got a newspaper and a cigarette and isn't looking our
way. (Thank goodness. I don't have a newspaper to hide
behind, and here she is waving this antenna deal around.
We're not exactly cloaked here.)

The announcement comes over loudspeakers: Running on time, arriving in ten minutes, the Texas Eagle to
Chicago.

"Okay, then." I sigh heavily for effect. "That's gotta be
where Arlene is. Let's go home and tell Lynwood."

"*Go home!* You miss the entire point. This is great."
She slides her palms back and forth against each other.
"No way could we stow away on a plane. Here, we're in
tall cotton."

Now she's talking like Grandmamma Ruby Rose. That means her sneaky brain is fully engaged. "Oh, no."

"You do not have to come," she informs me, turning away.

OMG. So many reasons not to do this come to mind that they overwhelm each other and I am in brainlock.

But I fire my best volley. "What'll happen when we don't come home for dinner? Lynwood will call out the cavalry."

She rolls her eyes. "I thought of that, airhead. Left them a note on the fridge where they'll see it when they take their tea-time vitamins. Said I was sure they remembered that today was the first day of Redbirds Sleepover Camp and we'd hitched a ride with Tara and her mom and we had packed everything and not to worry. That we'd call every night and report in."

No wonder she didn't carp about how long I took getting my stuff (while I was casting the cantrip): she wasn't just getting water bottles, after all.

She cracks her knuckles and looks absently at them as if surprised they'd made a noise. "You know Gary was all enthusiastic about us getting to go hiking and in the swimming hole and all that. Learning to tie knots and make lanyards or whatever. He'll be thrilled—he'll remember paying the rec center without checking to see when the camp actually is."

It's true: Gary does think we need more kid time. Doesn't believe the every-other-Saturday gig we have climbing the fake rock wall at Indoor Canyons and then going to Fargo's Pizza with the homeschool crowd is enough. He feels we need to be socialized by hanging out with our peers and all that rot. If only he knew our peers. If he did, he'd tell us to haul butt like the Road Runner.

"Clever. I bet they'll buy that. At least for a couple of days, until Lynwood calls the camp director to check whether you are taking your allergy pills and finds out the camp isn't even open this week." It's only late May, and there are several school districts still in session. The camp actually runs sometime in mid-June, if I remember correctly.

She shrugs. "I promised Arlene that if she needed me, I'd be there." She gazes into the distance like Joan of Arc with a Calling. "I may break rules, but never a promise."

I start counting money out of my pockets and purse. No time to hit the bank, and, besides, they'd report any withdrawals to Lynwood, as our account is joint and she's the adult on it.

"Never mind the small change. We're just going to hop on without tickets. We'll sneak back on among the smokers who get off to have a quick puff or two. I've read all about how to do it on the Amtrak Forums."

This is a sin. And a crime. I am certain of it. My innards start quaking as I step back, finding my knees weak. "We can't."

"Shut up, Cru. You'll see—we got off the DART train and we are already on the platform." She actually takes me by the shoulders and leads me over to one of the benches closer to the tracks. "Normally you buy your ticket and you pass through the station onto the plat-

form. That's how they control who gets near the train."
She pushes me down to sit on the bench. "But we are
already on the platform. So if we simply loiter a while
and don't go inside, we'll be on the platform and we
won't be asked for tickets until the conductor makes his
rounds. By then, we'll be hidden on the train."

Is her reasoning sound? I don't know.

"It's like in *North by Northwest*, sort of." She knows my
favorite films. "You know, when Eve hides Cary Grant
because she trusts he is on the side of the angels."

"Except we can't sleep with somebody."

"Speak for yourself." June settles in next to me exactly as if we're hillbillies waiting for Uncle Dennis to
arrive from Oklahoma City. Throwing a smug smile
to passersby for effect, she fans herself with the Amtrak
schedule she's picked up someplace. "The train has a
twenty-minute layover here, according to the sked. Includes a smoking break for passengers." She crumples
the brochure into a pocket on her laptop bag. "So just
sit tight."

this train is bound
for glory

June pulls out her laptop. She has ways of hacking into WiFi for free, and she does it now. I think there's a set of default passwords that IT types neglect or forget to change, and she has them memorized.

I haven't got the heart to pull out my tablet or laptop. Not only would it hamper a quick getaway if the need should arise, but also I know Gary's credit card is charged for the AirCard access by the minute. And that's traceable (credit card companies monitor your account for unusual activity, such as someone running up a bunch of minutes on an AirCard that's typically unused, and they often phone the cardholder immediately.) I'll save it for emergencies.

"We should buy a ticket. It's not right, sneaking on."

"Hush." She types a few characters quietly. "You're lucky I didn't stuff you in my rolling suitcase, steal Lynwood's VISA, buy one ticket, and smuggle you on the train."

"Don't be ridiculous. I'm too big to go in a suitcase and I couldn't breathe and you've seen too many sitcoms. Besides, Lynwood's VISA is probably run up to the hilt." We both know Gary watches his balances like a vulture waiting for something to rot, because he's so afraid of identity theft.

"So shut up already. We're fine. We'll figure it out. Don't be such a bundle of nerves." She has found the webpage she desires. It's all about the Dark Powers and how to contact them.

I hope the page is a put-on and not for real. I mean, surely going over to the Dark Side is at least as complex as becoming a Catholic, where you have to go to CCD and learn the catechism and then you get initiated, I mean confirmed, or the A. M. E. church where we attended a few times with the nanny we used to have and got ourselves baptized to great fanfare (after which time Lynwood decided it was up to us whether or not to go to church, and we preferred to stay home and lounge.) It's not something you decide to do as a lark.

The Dark Powers are (apparently) for real and not to be trifled with. My sister, as usual, thinks she is better than me at everything, and apparently she has taken off on one of her sudden quests for knowledge, inspired by my finesse with the grimoire. But she's mostly a poser, and I hope she doesn't get us noticed by Something Nasty with her fooling around. I'm sure you can't just pick and choose this or that to believe, like magic was a Chinese menu on two-for-one night.

Besides, without some kind of guidance, like a priest or mentor or whatever, it would be terribly, terribly dangerous to initiate yourself and mess with spellcasting.

I know, I'm one to talk. Still, the book talked to me. I didn't go looking for trouble.

I've thought of something else. "What's going to happen when the perp sees us here in a minute?"

"He won't. We're moderately disguised, and I did cast a spell to keep him away from us." She sighs theatrically. "I only hope I chose the proper sacrifice."

She'll be flattered if I quiz her about what she's supposedly learned. "Why did you have to sacrifice anything at all?"

I can hear the eyeroll in her tone. "Cru. Please. Magic, like anything else worth doing, has a cost. Just be grateful this had a rather trivial requirement in regard to material components."

I didn't need any material sacrifice with the cantrip. There is no point in questioning her further, as the whistle and the chugging overtake everything. The train is pulling in. The moment it stops, a line of people pours off and they all light up.

Apparently the online site was right about this stop being a smoking break.

A knot of mostly younger people forms near us, smoking and staring at downtown Dallas.

June stands up and stretches. I envision her pulling out a cigarette and starting to pretend-puff away, even though she has never smoked ANYTHING as far as I know.

"What are we doing?" I whisper, hoping she gives me a clue.

"Leave it to me," says June.

Even as she blows me off, she sits bolt upright. I follow her gaze to the glint of a wheelchair. An older lady, apparently in need of the chair (at least for now), is being assisted aboard by red-jacketed Disability Mobility Team Members.

"Here's our chance. Come on." She jerks me to standing and practically drags me behind her like a pull-toy. We get in line behind the lady. She is half of a harried couple about the right age to be our grandparents, and the train men actually help boost me up as if we're with them. Once on, we take a turn the opposite way down the corridor, June shouting as if to the "grandparents" that we're finding the ice and water station.

And then we hide in the toilet. Which is bite-sized, a one-seater. Our contortions as a result are out of every slapstick movie ever. We huddle down together, clutching our backpacks on our knees, and pray silently (at least I do) that no one will check the place. I can hear murmurs as the conductor is conducting business with the roomettes along the hall. When the train starts moving, June peeks out the door.

"Coast is clear," she says. "Wait here."

I can't hide in the bathroom until she comes back, whenever that might be. In the hallway I grab at her arm, but she shakes me off and heads towards a car full of empty seats. There's a nook nearby where you can get free bottled water and other sundries, so I skulk over to fool around with cups of ice. In a few minutes June appears and presses a stub of paper into my palm.

"What's—"

"Seat pass. Proves you belong on the train. Now, let's go."

For a moment I'm confused, but then I realize that people must leave their passes in their empty seats when they make a run for drinks and such. She probably looked up what to steal on the net on some train fancier's site. I hope this doesn't inconvenience some legit passenger. Before I can protest (even if I could work up the guts to do it), June is making her move, so I follow like a meek lemming.

We hurry back down to where the private roomettes should be. I saw on the train's floor plan that the wheelchair-accessible bedroom is at the end of the car. June knocks and pulls the accordion door aside without waiting for an answer.

The family roomette is larger than I thought it would be, and occupied by a twinkly-eyed grandfather (a Santa type) as well as the walker-bound lady we saw earlier.

When June breathlessly explains, they agree to let us stay in there with them. Except of course June does not explain the *truth*, but her version of truth.

"We're on our way to visit our dad. We haven't seen him for nearly a year." With that bandana and that innocent expression, June manages to pass for a younger girl. I nearly believe her myself. "Mother put us in Coach and we've come all the way from Los Angeles." She lies so easily. "Across the mountains and the desert, sitting in seats, and we're just so tired. My legs cramp." She winces for effect.

"That's very dangerous, dear. You can get deep thrombosis—that's blood clots." The lady frowns and pats my sister on the calf.

"Y'all are so lucky. You can stretch your legs in here." She usually doesn't drop down into country Texan talk unless she's really turning on the charm. The theater is missing out on a true diva.

"You must be so tired."

June regards me fondly, as if she actually cares whether I'm in pain or not, which generally isn't her main concern. "My sister is even more tired than I am."

The old man winks at me, but not in a pervy way; it's the way grandpas and uncles do to let you know they're on to you but they're not going to tell. "Y'all set a spell. You look exhausted."

"How far you going?"

"All the way to Chicago. Daddy lives in that building where the *Bob Newhart Show* characters supposedly lived on the shore of Lake Michigan."

"Well, dear, that's a long way. Why don't you get on the bunk and lie down for a while? We'll cover for you. I suspect they won't bother us at any rate, because they already have our bunks opened out and everything's cozy."

June shoots me a look. "Thank you so much. I know my sister's exhausted."

This is my cue to curl up and look pathetic. It's not tough at all.

"My GPS says we're going a hundred miles an hour," June is saying about an hour later, as I am jolted awake by a particularly rough stretch of track. She is showing the gadget to the old people and they are delighted with her techie skills and her explanation of geocaching ("I use multi-million dollar satellites to find Tupperware hidden in the woods with gumball-machine trinkets inside, and then I open it and write a poem on the log and I win prizes by posting about it on the Internet.")

"You will grow up to do great things, I predict, dear," the old lady says, patting her on the head. (June tolerates this, which is a surprise.) "Become some kind of computer programmer, I'll bet."

They're naïve for their age.

We are taking advantage of them. They're like the grandparents I barely know and it gives me guilt pangs.

The only reason I am doing this is because I have to stay with June, keep an eye on her, not get separated. What do I have to worry about, anyway—oh not much really, except that Arlene is in trouble and this guy has maybe put out a contract on her and it's up to us to stop him, plus we are defrauding the railroad and lying to these nice old people to boot. How could I have dozed off?

I've got to be sure Santa took the cookies—that is, I must make certain the parental units bought June's crazy note. I flash on Lynwood down at the downtown Renner DART station finding our bikes locked to the racks and fainting into Gary's arms, whereupon he sweeps her up and runs to the police station where he starts filing all sorts of Missing Teenagers reports.

I wonder whether I can get away with calling home from my smartphone, or could the cops trace that? I've heard the government tracks people to within thirty feet. It could be true. Would it matter? I mean, would anybody check? Probably not right away. On the other tentacle, if Lynwood actually answered, I'm not sure I could pull off the illusion of being at camp instead of on a train rocketing towards Chicago.

"Excuse me for a moment. I need to powder my nose," I say at the first lull in the conversation.

"If you need the restroom, dear," says our hostess, "it's just down the corridor at the other end of the car. On the left."

I always marvel when people use this kind of "if" clause. I mean, if I didn't want to use the restroom, then where would it be? Still down the corridor, or absent completely, or undecided, like that cat in the science experiment?

But anyway, I thank her and scurry down the hall to the observation car. It doesn't take long to develop the shipboard gait that I need to navigate the swaying corridor with the clack of the rails underneath my feet.

The lights of the night city are far away. Twilight has overtaken dusk. Cow pastures are visible out the windows on both sides of the train. We must be somewhere in Arkansas. I open TweetyBird, knowing who'll be on at this time of night. I can only hope he likes me the way I think he does.

I send him a tweet.

#APRILCOMESHEWILL => #JUSTIN_TIME: Hey, I need a favor. Please tell Lynwood or Gary that you saw me hiking today.

In a moment bright letters scroll across the smartphone screen.

#JUSTIN_TIME: Who is this? Never mind, "I remember April." *grin* What's up?

#APRILCOMESHEWILL: Say you saw me with June up at Cliffwood Ridge on the nature trail with the Redbird troop at noon. That we looked tired but happy. Take along a book as an excuse and tell them you borrowed it, and seeing us reminded you to return it. Go see them now, before dark, please?

After a moment I get a return tweet.

#JUSTIN_TIME: OK — will do

#JUSTIN_TIME: Where are you really?

#APRILCOMESHEWILL: Can't explain right now. Just please go knock right away and act like you're surprised you saw us. But that we seemed great. Need them not to worry.

#JUSTIN_TIME: Be careful, you two

#APRILCOMESHEWILL: Thanks.

There's a pause, and then he types:

#JUSTIN_TIME: G'nite — sleep safe

I feel my face burning. That was downright forward of me, but I had no choice but to ask him. What's the use of blushing if he can't see me? Nothing to display embarrassment for in here except the odd dozing-off traveler and the blank face of the night windows.

Our parents are just clueless and flaky enough to accept that Justin would spot us out there and would think to ask them about it because we're well-known homebodies. They trust him because they know he's a neighbor kid. And Lynwood made a huge commission by selling his parents that house a couple of years ago, so of course she loves them. I have to congratulate myself for thinking of this.

I call Lynwood's cell instead of the house landline because I know she'll ignore it if she's deep in concentration, which she will be because at this time of day she's watching "Singing With the Superstars." Sure enough, it clicks over to voicemail.

"Yeh," I say in the sleepiest tone I can manage — which isn't too tough — "we're out here sleeping in cabins that look like something abandoned in World War Three. But there aren't any bedbugs and I took a shower. I'm tired and June is a lump of misery from our hike on the ridge, but we're fine. My other cabinmates are cool. Tomorrow we get to swim. Love you; call you tomorrow. Probably late, because they make us leave our phones in the cabin so we can have the wilderness experience." I think this is a nice touch. "G'nite. Oh, and I made you a lanyard."

There. That should be good for a few hours of her smiling gently to herself. She's proud that we function as self-actuating individuals. I send up a prayer asking forgiveness for the lies, although I don't repent of lying, so the prayer probably goes unheard. If you really need to tell a white lie, does it count as a sin?

I guess what with casting magic spells and all one little lie doesn't matter; I'm definitely on iffy ground spiritually. Whatever. I just like to keep my lot thrown in with the saints.

I snap the phone closed and head back down the corridor. After a moment's thought, I take the battery out of the phone and put it in my jacket pocket. I've heard that the police can find your cell phone through GPS if it's on, and I don't want to take chances. June has undoubtedly taken hers apart already, as I haven't heard it ring and haven't seen her consulting it, which she usually does fairly often.

Frantic calls and wild-eyed e-mail messages from our parents will start bouncing fairly soon, I predict. My voicemail fills up fast.

While I'm flying solo, I take advantage of the facilities and grab a couple of plastic cups of ice and two mini water bottles. Not just because they're free or because my mouth is as parched as an elephant's belly button. This gives me an excuse as to why I took so long.

But I don't need one. They're all deep in conversation still. Rather, June is talking and they're listening indulgently. Sometimes she doesn't know when she's being boring, but they were raised in the olden days with good manners, or maybe they're just starved for young people's company, so they're pretending to listen with rapt attention. I manage to check June's phone (dead as a dirt clod, without one battery bar) as I take off my shoes to stash them next to her pack, and then I get comfy again in the top bunk where I can have a modicum of privacy.

The lady is now briefing June on how to live in general. "I was too worried when I was your age. Now I don't care what people think. Just be happy. And be nice, because everyone will forget what you said or did, but they never forget how you made them feel. Good manners are free."

It's sad if these people don't have grandchildren, presuming they don't, because they'd be great at it.

Grandpa-man tosses one of those fuzzy throws and a sheet over me as I stretch out. My own pack serves as a pillow. I can't let the book stray far from me during the night, after all. Checking in with it under the covers, I find nothing but an Amtrak timetable. It thinks it's so witty. But my extra clothing makes my pack almost tolerable as I settle my head on it.

This still doesn't feel right. I dig out Nana's New Testament and tuck it into my front breast pocket. In battles, books like this one have deflected bullets. Not that we're looking at physical bullets, but I figure spiritual ones are just as bad. Worse.

I drift into that murky territory between waking and sleep as June starts explaining the Internet (her version) to the elderly couple. Outside the train windows the world is rolling up the sidewalks as the sky darkens.

I finally doze off, rocked in the arms of the Cannonball.

the jumping-off point

The sunlight pouring through the blinds, along with the stirrings of my co-passengers, wakes me early. June must have slept on the top couch with me feet-to-head and then crept out again without my even hearing her, because she's already awake and pacing in the cramped quarters. Our little old lady is stirring a cup of hot coffee and our little old man still dozes in his bunk. I have the manners to thank the woman profusely as I get re-shod and shoulder my pack.

June's already scheming, as usual. "We really appreciate your letting us stay with you. But we'd better go back to our seats in case the conductor is watching for

us. He knows we are traveling without our parents. I
signed up for the breakfast call at eight-fifteen."

She is so confident. And such a smooth liar. What's
another little sin?

We pass through the coach car. Even as she palms a
couple of abandoned seat passes, June is lecturing me
out of the corner of her mouth. "Careful what you pick
up. We wouldn't want to be stuck with an RFID."

"Okay. What's an RFID? Re-Fried Icky Doughnut?
Regular Flavor Intelligent Dorito? Rotten Foul Ink
Dot?"

June snorts because I am So Impossibly Ignorant.
"Come on, Cru. You know those radio frequency iden-
tification tags that are imbedded in your driver's license?
They're on all sorts of stuff. There is a whole theory
about tracking people by putting RFIDs in shoes. The
ultimate is the chips they put in your body, like they do
in pets." She tilts her head. "Trains have them, and there
are chip readers along the track. That way, the dispatch-
ers know where trains are at all times, and the speed, and
all that. Kind of cool, actually. I wonder what qualifica-
tions you need to be a dispatcher? Burlington Northern
has a central office in Fort Worth."

June iterates through possible professions like a chan-
nel-surfer through the cable networks. But she'd be
bored instantly once she actually got one of these jobs, I
am sure.

We head for the observation car where they sell
snacks. "I'm perturbed because I haven't seen Arlene's
supposed boyfriend," I complain.

"Stinktongue?" Apparently she has her own nickname for him. "I did. I saw him get on."

"But not since then." I'm worried that he gave us the slip sometime during the night. There were brief stops all along our route all night that I could feel as the train squealed to a halt and then accelerated again.

"Cru, we were in a stateroom," she says in a reasonable tone. "Hey, they page people to the dining car when their reservation time comes along. Maybe he'll get paged. ZONTAR THE MAGNIFICENT, DE-STROYER OF WORLDS, AND RAPER OF INNO-CENCE: your Frappucino is ready."

I almost laugh. But it strangles in my throat as I spot the guy. "Look, there he is." I grab June's arm. "In the dining car, the first booth just beyond the door. Careful, he's facing us."

He's looking at the menu, not at us. Still, his sudden (to us) appearance seems to make June nervous. She steps backwards onto my toes.

My *OUCH* is muffled as she claps her hand over my mouth.

The noise is also covered by a train-speaker announcement. "Next stop, St. Louis, Missouri. Twenty-minute layover."

Stinky glances our way. June practically spins on her tiptoes and drags me deeper into the coach car, all in one motion. She can move fast when she needs to. Stepping on toes and "excuse-me"-ing all the way, we speed into the observation car, where there are too many people for him to be able to attack us, if he's seen us.

He's standing up. He's headed this way.

Catching her breath, my sister sets her face to reflect total boredom. We hurry to the next car. I paste on the "wish I were anywhere but here" look of a typical teenager. He's still coming.

Stepping backwards in unison, we find we're standing in front of someone's empty single roomette. By the time the bad guy strides past, we're scrunched together inside it. June is so scared she doesn't even rifle the compartment for the morning paper or loose change. We wait until the corridor is quiet.

"Let's go back to the observation car." Taking my finger out of my mouth now that the cuticle is totally shredded, I'm ready to give up this pursuit right NOW. I think it was Nana's New Testament—or at least Someone Up There watching over us—that put this empty roomette at our disposal. We don't need to tempt fate any further.

"We have to bring this to an end. Don't you want to rescue Arlene?"

"I don't really see how we're helping her if we get ourselves killed."

Her expression tells me I'm talking crazy.

My head spins for a moment. "How can we be sure he's going after Arlene himself? Maybe Stinky's going to visit his parents. On a job interview. To meet a chick he knows from the Internet."

"Just follow my lead. Do what I do." She cocks her head as if listening. "I think he's gone into his room. Stand on one leg and lean ahead to see."

I do not know why I do what my sister says.

"He's not in the hall any more," I report.

"Okay." Her exhaled breath could fill ten balloons. "All right, then. We're safe if we confront him. We'll have the upper hand. He can't kill or hurt us because there are too many witnesses." I can only hope that trope (garnered, probably, from repeated viewings of *Murder, She Wrote*) is true. "I have pepper spray on my key chain."

Such a comfort. She arms herself with it, and I only hope her finger doesn't slip. Is that a bead of sweat on her brow?

June closes her eyes. "Let's take a moment to center ourselves and get grounded."

"We're already grounded for life, ha ha."

"Shhh. Focus."

I seek my inner center the way Lynwood taught us to do in meditation, and then peek out of the corner of my eye to see how June is "grounding." She looks like a fist, face and hands completely clenched. Completely ground to a fine powder, that's us. But in a moment her eyes open. "Let's roll."

She heads downhall with me on her heels. We get to his roomette and she brandishes the pepper spray canister. She flings open the magnetic door dramatically, without knocking. "We meet again," she says in her James Earl Jones voice.

But there's a minor problem.

Sprawled across the seat is a yellowing skeleton, still clad in the Dark One's outfit. No flesh, no blood, no debris in the room or on the bones. His clothing appears untouched, except for the sneakers, where the leather and rubber hung off the naked footbones. His hands, stretched out as if to shield himself, have been degloved and laid bare, like the rest of him. It looks like some Halloween decoration was tossed carelessly in here. The only part of him remaining is his face, an oblong human mask from chin to forehead, left intact though already darkening, with his staring eyes revealing shock and surprise. It smells vaguely of bad hamburger after a night in the Dumpster.

"He's lost a lot of weight," I gasp out, coping by zinging the first stupid joke that floats into my mind, but June's expression doesn't get any less terrified.

June takes a step back, her heels right against my ankles. We bang heads and shout, although she muffles me with both hands and clamps her lips closed. We back into the corridor, but no one seems to be responding. Thinking we're typical screechy teen girls, I suppose.

She jerks the door closed behind her. "The way he looks," June says quietly in a raw voice, "I know it was a magical kill."

"You don't *know* that," I whisper, "but I'll bet it's a fricking good guess." Magical kill, huh. She must be going by the movies she has seen, the ones I was deemed "too young" to view. Although what else could have consumed his flesh? Not your run-of-the-mill mugger. Awful as this is, it appears to have spurred June to fully embrace the concept of magic.

"Does he have any ID?"

June ducks back in there as though to check. She emerges after a moment, obviously shaken. "I couldn't stand to touch anything. So he might, or might not."

"I'm glad you didn't touch him. Fingerprints. The powers killed him, but we will be the suspects." I wheeze.

She blinks. "Cru, how could we have done it?"

"How could anyone?" I spread my palms. "But even if they think it's a fake, a prank, they'll ask questions. We were seen standing here. And we're flying under the radar."

"People have been detained for less." June's forehead furrows, which it never does.

My throat is so dry I can barely rasp out my thoughts. "We aren't just in deep doo-doo, we're in a pothole inside the Marianas Trench." I think I am having trouble breathing.

She yanks her old asthma inhaler out of her pocket. "You're wheezing. Take a hit."

There's just enough left for one puff.

"And of course it's obvious that he was killed because he was headed to find Arlene. Isn't it?" June raises her brows.

Maybe not, but my heartbeat is a drum solo and I can't get enough air yet. All I know is that we've been seen tracking him around the train. There will be questions, and I have no answers.

June, however, does have answers, as usual. "If magic killed him, then magic must also know we are trailing him. Somebody—or something—knows we were on to him and that we're following him so we can save Arlene."

I nod. Then the implications of her deduction hit me. "And therefore, it's logical to assume that we are also targets. Which means we...might wind up as skeletons any minute now." The idea sends a caterpillar up and down my spine, and I clutch at the wall for support.

She just looks at me as if I am the first-grader who jumped up and yelled, "I get it! Fire is hot!"

"You know what we have to do," my sister says.

"Leap off the train into the weeds, like in the movies?"

"No, clueless one. I do not want us to break any bones." She nods as if to herself. "We'll get off at the smoke break and wander into the station at St. Louis. Then we will wait for the next Eagle to Chicago because that is where he was evidently going." She looks pensive. This means she is up to something.

I am so nutter-butter that I'm beside myself (the cliché describes this mental state pretty well). "The porter or whoever is sure to come by. And they'll look in here."

"No, they won't. Here's the do-not-disturb signal; I've been paying attention." She steps back in to pull the black drapes across the windows that open to the corridor. Then, cool as can be, she steps out and pulls his magnetic folding door all the way across and closed. She grins like a teenybopper at a man passing by, who nods and smiles. Nice teenagers, innocent and helpful.

We make our way toward the front of the car, where we stashed our stuff earlier. June and I perch on the exit stairs behind the smoking crew; they already have their

lighters and cigs out and are twitching to get out and
fire up. When the train slows, I can feel everyone tens-
ing. It's like we're the rear paws of an ocelot preparing
to pounce.

As soon as it stops we're all outta there.

st. louis blues

Lots of jazz musicians hail from St. Louis. It wasn't the birthplace of the blues, but it was an intermediate rest stop on the way up the Mississippi from New Orleans to Chicago. So it's the proper place for me, as I am fast developing a major (not minor, ha) case of the blues.

Gateway Station in East St. Louis is not as big as their historic Union Station, but is still large. It's next to the Greyhound bus depot, with a Mondrian-like stained-glass skywalk connecting the two buildings. I can see the famous Busch Stadium as the train pulls slowly in.

We jump down from the exit stairs with the trembling smoker fiends and stride into the depot as if we belong there. It's bustling with people, some of whom look particularly seedy. But there are also businesspeople. And the place smells like any school, like disinfectant and grease traps. The midday sun streams in through several windows onto the seating area.

June pulls an exaggerated yawn and stretches her arms, twirling a couple of times. I sidle up to the counter and collect brochures about the area, along with a train schedule, from the rack. She sits down on a bench in the corner sunbeam and acts like we're just where we need to be.

"So now what?"

"I don't know yet, but have faith." June twists her ring. It really sparkles in that sunbeam.

My worrywart mode kicks in. If my ruse about camp and hiking didn't work, or if Lynwood got suspicious and phoned the camp, then there is almost definitely an Amber Alert out for us by now. Even progressive parents like ours go nuts when young girls disappear. Time is of the essence.

But all I say aloud is, "We can't afford to stay here long. We need to get on to Chicago."

"But not on that particular train. It only runs every two days, according to this. Other trains don't leave until like three in the morning, and we can't wait that long, as you said." She taps the schedule against her chin. "Maybe we'll hitch."

"Too dangerous."

June barks out a laugh. "Compared to what we've already done?" Then she reconsiders. "You might be surprised," she says vaguely. She pulls a black leather wallet out of her pocket.

Realization dawns on me like ten pounds of oh-no-she-didn't. "You stole his wallet? You said you couldn't bear to touch him."

"I lied." Her lips curl upwards.

My sister rolled a corpse. One who was magically murdered.

"He didn't need this any more." She sounds utterly reasonable. "I think we'll find clues here to where Arlene is." She begins sorting through cards out of the wallet's slots. She's already pulled out three twenties. "Driver's license in the name of George Willard. Obviously a fake name. It's out of that old Sherwood Anderson book that Gary was so hot for us to read last year, until Lynwood convinced him we were too young to understand that garbage." She smirks because she knew that. "No credit cards, but it'd be too risky to use them anyhow. Here's a StarBaby coffeeshop gift card, though."

She has moved on past his death, but I haven't. Is there something wrong with me—or with her? Should I pray for him? Involuntarily I cross my arms over my chest and squeeze, feeling a shiver again.

Across the street is a StarBaby coffeehouse. In a few minutes June announces she is hungry and we head over. She has a bit of trouble getting the barista's attention, which I think is an effect of the Unnoticeable working.

It seems that we can get someone's attention if we want it, but if we don't, we're fairly well ignored, which is nice.

June pulls her usual get-one-free schtick.

"I'd like a half-caff mint mocha soy latte with three left-handed squirts of sugar-free vanilla syrup and two of caramel mocha. Oh, and chocolate chips, please." June gets her really elaborate order and takes one sip, then does a spit-take. The barista guy makes her another one with only two left-handed squirts, and she says it's STILL not quite right. She makes the fish face of pouting. By the time there are two rejected tall paper cups sitting before her on the countertop, she's nearly crying. "Can I talk to your manager?"

The barista, apparently having had trouble before with mean, whiny customers, glances furtively around. "Sorry, she's gone on an errand. But here, have a free cookie. On me. On the house."

She reaches over and palms two prewrapped behemoth Snickerdoodles without getting caught. Then she pays for the second coffee with her stolen gift card, and when the barista is distracted, she surreptitiously latches on to the first cup as well, snagging it in kind of the same way I imagine an old-style locomotive grabbed the mail using the hook without stopping in the Old West. She stomps over to a booth by the window.

Snagging the second cookie out from in front of June, I plop down across from her. She only glares at me a little.

The cookie is on the near edge of stale, but I need something to keep my blood sugar up. The drink isn't bad, either.

June rubs her forehead with both palms. "Do you have any aspirin?"

I begin pawing through my backpack looking for the bottle I know I have, pulling out random items. A Barbie-style fashion doll clatters to the table, and her jaw drops. Before I can retrieve it, she grabs it. Instantly she's so freaked she can't even sneer. "What the hell are you doing with a Bunny doll? You still play with Bunny and Kenny?"

Uh-oh.

"That's a video-recording Bunny doll. Remember, Aunt Jean sent it to me last year. She thinks I'm perpetually six years old." I can't keep the note of defensiveness out of my voice. "I hung on to it because it does have a fairly good digital camera. Disguised as Bunny's pendant." I clutch at the hollow of my throat to indicate the camera's location. "You can turn it off and on with the remote control, so it's a functional spy-cam. It's not as lame as you're thinking. Anyway, I forgot it was even in my pack."

Her expression slowly changes. "Okay, then, that's different." Turning the doll back and forth in her hand, she zones out for a minute.

It's unnerving. "Wake up. Your eyes are glazed over like the most fattening doughnut."

She comes to her senses and tosses the doll back to me. "Keep it. Might come in handy."

Repacking my bag, I still don't find the aspirin. I do find my makeup (poor neglected toolbox) and mini sewing kit complete with thimble, among other odds and ends. All the necessities of modern life. Except the one June wants.

She's flipping through websites on her laptop.

"Why can't I find anything," June says to no one in particular. "An immunity-from-magic spell, ideally. But I'm not finding it." She chews her lip thoughtfully, looking at a new splash page. "Maybe *this* would be OK. No, too many possible side effects."

It disturbs me that she's gone off on one of her tangents, this time with magic as her new obsession (to replace tattoos), because a little knowledge with no guidance can dig you a pretty deep hole. On the other hand, I'm relieved that she's thinking ahead again. No sense risking side effects, like maybe some spell that lets you fly like Superman, except the danger is that it occasionally turns you to liquid. Splashing down into someone's pool as a glob of slime is definitely not my thing.

She retreats behind the laptop screen for a bit while I finish my cookie and caffeine fix and consult the brochures I found. "There's a drugstore not far from here. Plus a college."

"And you're telling me this because...?" She doesn't look up from her laptop.

"I just thought that might be someplace better to hide. From the bad magic, or other possible dangers. Lot of people our age, so we'd blend in." I shrug. "The campus must be nearby. A few blocks, tops. I could get a map online." Actually, I already have one showing on the smartphone screen. A few blocks and we'd be there.

She doesn't answer.

Surreptitiously I consult the grimoire. It has a film-strip all ready for me, which starts when I open to the first page, like a cartoon playing on a placemat. It shows June and me in a nondescript-looking shop, then climbing onto a bus. A bus?

No words are forthcoming, only pictures. It shows the bus traveling fast, then fades to black. I've noticed it hardly ever tells me something that's going to be immediately relevant, so I file this away for later.

"Where is Arlene?" I ask it under my breath. It doesn't deign to answer.

"How does this work," I ask the book. "What is magic?"

It does the bit with the fancy Ben Franklin quill, stylized letters flowing across the page, this time in tangerine orange.

Magic workings access the Unseen Forces that hold this World together and restrain the influence of Other Worlds beyond the Barriers that have been set by the Same Forces.

Oh.

More spidery writing appears, but I am in no mood to talk metaphysics in general. "Thank you," I tell the book, "that's all I can take for now." Genius or no genius, I'm getting tired and worried and I want to get this over with.

"Let's go," I say to June as I close the grimoire firmly (with the suspicion that it is still busily scribing away) and secrete it into the backpack. I need to rearrange some stuff to make room, and that stupid Bunny doll keeps getting in the way.

"Okay, okay." She practically slams her laptop and stuffs it back into her bag. Swinging her legs out of the booth before I can even get my bag zipped, she says, "Come on, then, we'll explore a bit. Get some aspirin at a drugstore. But I don't think we should fool around too long. We need to figure out how we're going to get to Arlene."

spelling lessons

I follow her a few blocks to a corner drugstore, where we stock up on aspirin and chewing gum. Next door to the pharmacy June's true destination reveals itself: an occult shop. I should've known this little errand was a ruse. Well, she *did* buy and take the aspirin. But still.

The book was misleading in its portrayal of the shop: this is no nondescript hole-in-the-wall. It's an exotic hole-in-the-fabric-of-mundanity.

Rough pine shelves fill the store, like in the old second-hand bookstore we used to haunt at home in Renner. But these shelves sag beneath the weight of giant glass jars containing dried herbs, baskets of polished stones, packets of powder, trinkets, statuary (ceramic, stone, and otherwise), thin candles (tapers, cut and uncut), fat candles (votives and pillars)—anything and everything you could imagine that a "practitioner" (which is what the subtle hand-lettered signs keep calling us) might want. And the heavenly scent! I breathe in a blend of clove, cinnamon, apple butter, hazelnut coffee, pumpkin pie, and lots of other yummy aromas—but I note that they're accompanied by a pungent undertone of licorice and wormwood, to let you know that not every talisman serves a positive purpose. Flickering candles, along with practical overhead fluorescents, light our way as June breezes past a display of books ("How to Turn Your Boss Into a Toad") and heads toward the more serious wares in the back.

There are a few displays that pull double duty as altars. These altars have obviously been dedicated to a particular saint, Pagan god(dess), or demon—pick your preferred spin on the entity. They feature burning candles, scrying bowls, sacred images or statues, and polished stones. I don't examine these too closely for fear something might zap me.

I would've expected an occult shop to have collected a lot of nasty negative energy from the voodoo customers and so forth, but I don't feel that at all. In fact, I don't know what I feel. Mostly trepidation (that's fear to you SAT-goons) about what my sister might get us into, but that twinge is an everyday experience for me.

The ethereal being behind the counter is wrapped in a veil of long blonde hair. She seems absorbed in sorting mystery capsules into different-colored cylinders. She doesn't look up, and June doesn't bother to ask where anything is. My sister simply heads for the long, crowded shelves.

My sister probably concocted a list of items she thinks we'll need from looking at a bunch of creepy webpages while I was snarfing the caffeine, although I know she'll root around and find things she didn't know she wanted. She picks up some sealing wax and a length of black satin ribbon. Green and orange votives. A peacock feather. Then she starts sorting through cones of incense in various scents. I'll bet we'll get into trouble if we start burning that stuff.

She snatches up a gross-looking piece of what looks like dried ginger root off a shelf. "I'm sure we'll need this."

I hold my nose. "It stinks."

June shoots me a dark glance. "All a matter of perspective. It's tannis root. Tannis is a Greek name from the Semitic word Tanith, meaning serpent lady. Tanith was a goddess of fertility."

So she's been reading the encyclopedia. Or she rewatched *Rosemary's Baby* recently. Either way, that stuff still stinks.

Examining my fingernails, I realize I haven't chewed my cuticles all day. That's a good sign. I've been too worried to gnaw on them, what with everything gnawing at me. "Are we ready to roll?" I ask empty air.

Because June has bounced over to the next aisle, where she gets matches with black sticks and red-violet heads. On an apparent impulse she picks up a couple of polished amethyst stones. Apparently she just likes their smooth feel and transparent purpleness, because she grins and pockets them.

Slipping things into her pocket without paying. I am not going to say a word about it. If the clerk peeks out from behind her curtain of hair and catches June in the act, it'll serve her right.

June glides to the checkout counter and digs the rest of the dead guy's cash from her little blue wallet. The clerk eyes us curiously. I suddenly get the vibe that this is not just an herbal apothecary and bookstore, but a religious shop, and this woman truly considers the collection of icons behind her to be a shrine. Milady rings up what June lays on the counter. She wraps our purchases in brown Kraft paper speckled with black pentacles and other weird occult symbols, binds the package up with rainbow ribbon, and then places it in a sack and hands it to June. "Be careful, girls."

"We're not *girls*." June tosses her hair rebelliously, forgetting it isn't there any more. "We're *young women*."

"Ah." The black candles behind the proprietress-presumably-also-sorceress flicker and one snuffs itself, although I don't feel any breeze. "Of course. So sorry. Take care, anyway."

Outside the shop, it's clearer that this is not the best part of town. A couple of knots of tough-looking people seem to be eyeing one another. Some of them begin gesturing, and I worry they might be flashing gang signals. It would be nice if we could get out of their line of fire. Fortunately, a steeple pokes up towards the clouds from a group of the college's buildings, barely a block away. The college chapel, probably in the middle of campus, a safe haven for us. I hope.

Steering June subtly in that direction, I discover I'm right. We follow a wide ribbon of rolling lawn to the group of buildings that I imagine makes up most of the campus. I manage to "turn my ankle" right in front of what looks like a dorm.

Wincing, I grab my leg. "Yow!" I plop onto a student-studded square of grass in front of the double doors. "Man, I think I screwed up my ankle."

This forces June to cave. "Okay, okay, we'll go in here. Maybe that'd be good. Wouldn't be a problem for me to sit down and think a while. If there's a common room, I can plug in the laptop and phone so they can recharge." She looks concerned and actually insists I lean on her arm as we proceed slowly through the building's glass doors.

It turns out that this is a dorm, but one that is currently very sparsely populated.

A janitor must be swabbing the floors somewhere down the long front hall, because the dorm smells like Pine-Sol. Doors are propped open along the hall's length, and several dorm rooms are bare except for the beds and desks. They might be empty for the semester, or maybe the brass wall plaque reading "Guest Quarters" indicates that this is a place for visiting parents and potential scholars to stay while they check out the campus.

"This is even better," June says. I figure our "Unnoticeable" spell must still be working, because no housemother or resident assistant has appeared, and no one at all has challenged us. The occult shop's clerk, of course, noticed us, but we weren't trying to creep past her. The spell is a Good Thing (assuming I'm correct).

Choosing at random, we slip inside the second room on the right. There's no sign of habitation. That's nice, because I'm going to need a bathroom soon.

June plops down on her stomach on one of the bunks as if we belong there. I am tired enough despite all the "rest" I supposedly got on the train that I follow suit on the other bed.

"We're potential students touring the campus," she murmurs.

"Yeah, that would be us: girl geniuses, heading off to college in our early teens." I'm too weary to sigh as I prop my "damaged" leg up on the pillow and rummage in my pack. I don't even know what I'm looking for. To save face, I pull out some lip gloss and slide it on my lips.

June pulls out her laptop. She's already managed to find an outlet for charging our electronics. "I've been doing some research to help figure out what's happening to Arlene," she announces, bringing the Web browser up. "Here's my take on it. She has betrayed the Powers. She made herself holy and consecrated herself to the service of some powerful entity, and then she broke the rules. Badly." She smirks at her own cleverness.

"This of course assumes the actual existence of powers not of this corporeal world, things outside most people's immediate experience, and of real entities that can be invoked and evoked, abracadabra."

"Exactly," my sister says, so obviously I have not been sarcastic-sounding enough. She raises up on her elbows. Her eyes glow with an unnatural light. "Among the powers and privileges she was granted was a language arcane. Oblique. Unlike everyday speech. The powers are not to be addressed directly or as though they're kids in your class. Some of their words are known only to the few who command entrance to the spirit world."

"I prefer it here, thanks."

She sticks out her tongue.

I have an idea regarding where we might get our own word of power. If the grimoire feels like cooperating, that is. We might be safer asking it for one, rather than just playing in whatever multiverse June is finding on the net.

Although first, I do need to run to the bathroom.

"My ankle's better," I announce for June's benefit. Even though it twinges as I stand on it. I was only faking. Or so I thought.

This suite is rather nice, with its own private bath. After doing my required business (which Gary calls "unavoidable delay"), I scrub my hands and arms up to the elbows and splash my face. I look fairly wrecked, even with lipgloss. But I don't think I could get away with a real shower. That'd probably attract attention because these old pipes surely groan and creak when asked to provide hot water. Best not to make any loud noises.

Back in the room, I perch cross-legged on the edge of my (ha) bunk.

"Criss-cross applesauce," June says automatically, as a charm against the cross-legged curse.

"Toast and butter," I reply without even thinking. It's an old ritual we have. But even if she's in a whimsical mood, I need to prevent June from doing something that could be really harmful. "Speaking of *toast*, I'm afraid that will be a good description of us if you find some dangerous spell online and use it without any coaching or testing. We'll be in a real *jam*."

She ignores my lame puns. "Quiet down, Cruelest. I need to learn a word of power so I can do a working that reveals Arlene's location to us."

Why not? We're in a dorm, unauthorized, where we don't need to call attention to ourselves. What's the problem with chanting an incantation and waving our hands over a stream of stinky incense?

Of course she has simply fixated on this "word of power" thing because it was in some of that jazz she read on the Web. I don't know what use such a word might be to us, let alone what sort of working we can or should do.

I never knew that spells were for sale on the Internet, but June navigates to a page that offers (in exchange for your credit card number) any kind of hex or curse. The sellers guarantee results. Yeah, right. June plows through all manner of capitalistic sales pitching in order to find the real stuff, which (of course) needs to be concealed from the casual gawkers.

"Here's something." She clicks.

I do not like what appears on her screen. Every link description on the search results page sounds fairly hazardous. There should be skull-and-crossbones icons on some of these.

June clicks on an icon for a potential spell. She reads the text aloud.

"Become part-demon. Warning: this spell is irreversible and could have some disastrous effects; the demons will be sure to use you to their advantage with or without your knowledge or consent, and make you do errands which could be hurtful to others—but you get to astrally project into Hell if you like."

"Let's skip that one."

She doesn't respond. She looks too interested for my comfort. I reach over her shoulder and tab past it.

A page of top-rated conjuring spells fills the screen. They boggle my mind. June sees potential in several of them and clicks around, making sure she only hits on the freebies.

One spell includes a step involving the tracing of Solomon's Seal on the sorcerer's right hip using sap from a maple tree combined with ten drops of your own arterial blood. June dismisses it as too complicated. "I think I can rule out anything where we have to shed blood," she says meditatively. "It's way too squicky."

I can't say I don't feel a sense of relief. Although I neglect to point out to her that we have no maple sap;

there's only one sap in here, and I'm it, ha. I'd like to argue with her over these arcane-sounding texts, if I had time. But mainly I'd like to remain in one piece.

I clear my throat. "We don't want to tempt the fates. Could I try a shortcut?"

After glancing out our doorway to confirm that the few people passing by up and down the hall aren't paying any attention to us, I leap up to close the door. Then I pull the grimoire out of its hiding place in my backpack. "This is what I think will work."

"Of course." She grabs it out of my hands as if it is *hers* and not mine. "Let's ask it how to find her." To the book she says, "Take us to Arlene. Where is Arlene? How do we get to her?"

Again spidery ink crawls across the page as if from a quill dragged by some flowery old-timey writer like Edgar Allan Poe.

You shall use the incense of incantation.

"Oh, that's right. They're attracted by incantatory poetry," I remind June.

"What the hell's incantatory poetry?"

I have no answer for her. "The book mentioned something about that to me before."

That gleam in her eye bodes ill, as I know from experience.

"All right, I can deal." She closes her eyes and raises her arms straight up. In an unnaturally gritty (remember Kim Carnes?) voice she intones, "Hail, Guardians of the Watchtowers of the Four Compass Points. Hail to the North Direction. To the South Direction. To the East. To the West." As she announces each direction, June faces that way.

We might brew up a magical storm. Actually, storms and magic have a lot in common. Both must abide by laws: storms, the laws of nature like gravity and temperature, and magic...rules that I don't know yet, though I am sure there are rules. Either phenomenon can wreak a lot of havoc.

She waves her right hand in the air, tracing some kind of glyph, although it leaves no contrail. The ring sparkles fit to bust. It might set off a seizure in susceptible types. "Hail, ye spirits. We invoke and praise thee as natural forces that control the unseen world beneath what is seen." She grabs the back of her neck with her left hand as if it has just twinged. "Ouch," she whispers in her normal voice. She rubs at her neck. I think tossing her non-existent hair must have caused a crick in her neck.

She tries her hand at incantatory poetry.

"Let fortune turn our way to keep obstacles at bay. Show us where to find Arlene, okay? We must find her in time. Um, so that we may deter this crime."

Her rhymes make me wince. Also, her hair is going frizz-bomb with static electricity. It's standing on end, making her look like that old comic strip character, "Nancy." The hair on her forearms follows suit. I don't know what kind of power she is raising, but apparently raising power is hair-raising, ha.

Now June's pupils are dilating. That could be a sign of pleasure, or it might be darker in here than I had realized, or she might be getting taken over by the spell.

Standing with the book in her grasp, she raises it over her head. Skipping like Forrest Gump, she circles the room, skirting the beds. She reverse-arches her back snakily, the way you do in yoga, and bends her knees. What is she doing, the limbo? Just as I'm about to make some smart remark (that is, as soon as I can come up with one good enough), she reaches over and snatches up that disgusting gnarled root.

"Here is your sacrifice, O Powers!" June squeezes the root in one hand and rubs it against the book in the other. She traces circles around her stomach with the end of the tannis root and presents it to the book again. She makes one final spin in the middle of the room, and then rushes to the window. Throwing it open, she shouts, "Gone!"

She hurls the root as hard as she can. Oh, my God, I hope she doesn't hit someone in the quad. That's all we need, for her to conk someone into a stupor. ("She Conks to Stupor" is another of Gary's favorite plays on words, using the title of some ancient old play.) But she lucks out and it apparently disappears. At least I can't see where its trajectory ended.

The powers couldn't have taken it. That isn't the way the sacrifice of material components works; the power just takes what it wants with a puff of orange smoke. Doesn't it?

"June," I begin, but she whirls and hisses at me, her claws out like a tigress. She needs to come back to reality, and now. She looks skyward and her eyes nearly roll back in her head. "It is done," she says meaninglessly. "Where is my sign?"

Suppressing the snappy answers that crowd my mind, I rush over to ease the window closed. "We've got to quiet down. We'll be thrown out of here."

She searches the book with a disappointed gaze. "But I need a sign from the Powers." Obviously there's nothing appearing on the pages.

I'm afraid this is getting out of hand. And the smell of that rotting potato-thingy out in the yard might attract even more attention than some crazy teenager incanting stuff to the four directions.

"Thanks, don't call us, and we won't call you," I tell her. "Your audition piece is definitely avant-garde. Now may I take a look at the book and see what we're supposed to do?"

She can't admit defeat, but she does seem to realize she's dabbling in a deeper well than she has a rope for. She sinks down on the foot of the bed, looking grim. "I guess you can try," she grumbles, tossing the book to me.

I barely rescue it from landing on the floor between the beds. "Careful!" I don't mean to be unkind to June, but she has no respect for other people's property or for books in general, now that e-books are becoming so popular. I'm still an archivist at heart; they may have gotten the library at Alexandria, but they're not getting mine. Paltry as it is.

"Don't mind her," I tell the tome. "She means well. May I see my cousin and what's happening to her?"

I open the book to the middle page.

It shows us a full-color painting, in the style of Van Gogh, of good old Asmodeus. The sorcerer from the train.

"He's dead," she says to the book as if it is going to answer.

"He *looked* dead," I correct automatically. After all, I like to get the details right. Like a Fair Witness saying, when she sees a white horse, "This side of the horse is white," instead of assuming anything more. "Maybe he wasn't. Although it sure smelled that way."

"I didn't smell anything but stale bubble gum and Play-doh." She looks pretty determined to believe that, so I don't argue. I just want to clear my head (possibly with bleach) and forget that whole scene. June's eyes light up. "Maybe that wasn't him. I mean the creature we were following wasn't even him, but a golem. Yeah, that's it. He's not really dead, and that was just a golem to lure us."

"What's a...oh, yeah, from Dungeons and Dragons." A golem is a zombie-thing out of Jewish legend that a sorcerer can construct out of clay and turn into a semblance of anyone he wants so it can do his bidding. I contemplate this for a moment, but dismiss it. Such a thing doesn't even have a skeleton, and it would be too much trouble and take too much time to build just to use on us. More likely, that was some plastic thing from a Halloween shop, and we were just idiots who were completely fooled. But as usual June is off to the races with the idea.

"He must have created the golem during the night as we slept, and kept it hidden in his roomette. Also, he probably had a spell on the thing to keep the porter out. All that took the energy wa-a-ay out of him and also used up a spell that he likely had stored. So he had to lie low and couldn't come after us without his magic. Maybe he just wanted to be sure that we got off the train. Wanted to throw us off the track. Ha, the train track." She smiles at her lame pun.

"So you think he will be on the next train? Well, we need to ride a bus."

"What?" My sister stares at me.

"We go on a bus. I saw it earlier." I'd picked up, in my wad of brochures from the train station, a bus schedule. "There are buses headed every which way. There is one to Chicago Union Station from here, in fact, leaving later tonight. But we have no discretionary funds for that. Even if we use the guy's sixty dollars."

"Faith," my sister repeats.

She bought some patchouli (which is Hindu for "poop stink") incense cones at the occult shop, along with a pint-sized brass burner that looks as if it were yanked out of the Arabian Nights stories. Setting the burner on our shared night table, she lights the incense, humming a tune straight out of *Bell, Book, and Candle*. I only wish she had a Siamese cat she could sing to, like Kim Novak does with Pyewacket in the flick, so the spell would have some chance of working properly.

The smoke wafts up toward the ceiling in a spiral that doesn't look quite right. I'm not sure what smoke is supposed to do when it's billowing out. I mean, this looks like a stack of foggy doughnuts piling up. Maybe it's the way the censer is shaped.

My sister breaks the silence. "Well?" She's staring at a black page.

Nothing. I don't get a picture or whatever, either. Suddenly I feel a mist on my face and forearms and it's not raining. It goes hot and then cold. My sister's eyes meet mine and for a moment I see fear in them. Then she nonchalantly says, "I think it worked. Let's get something to eat."

Does that mean the sign for guidance will come later? I guess so.

I gather up the remnants of the material components, which she has strewn all over the bedspread, and stuff them into my pack because we ought to leave nothing but footprints. Not even footprints, if possible, in fact.

As for her spell, I can't say yet. So far, the only thing I've learned is that you can never be sure where you stand with magic. Nor can you ever know for sure if you've really done anything or if you were just playing.

The smoke alarms begin shrieking all down the hall. Apparently the university was prepared for this eventuality. There must be a lot of alarms going off on Saturday nights when the pot smokers are partying.

June hurriedly snuffs the incense and dumps the ashes so she can re-stow her burner. "Ouch!" Apparently the brass is still hot. But she has one of those coated wraps you use on the still-warm end of your curling iron so you can pack it immediately, so she gets everything safely put away in a jiff.

I shove my feet back into my shoes. They're both getting ripe.

A horde of irritated, muttering students is already shuffling out of the building, complaining about "yet another false alarm." In all the commotion, we lose ourselves easily in the crowd. This is one time when following the crowd is a Good Thing.

I follow June into what turns out to be the student center. Nobody's in there and the flatscreen is playing an unadmired re-run of some teenybopper reality show. I smell chili simmering on the steam table at the snack bar and June is starving. She's got that cash, so she just gets in line. As usual, she gets a Dagwood Bumstead-style club sandwich advertised as being made with "turkey ham." I never eat that stuff, because the term always makes me visualize a flightless flying pig that I'd love to have as a pet.

The food doesn't look too bad, and it seems like ages since I've eaten, so I slam down a tray and pick out a couple of egg rolls and some banana pudding.

I know I'm eating on stolen money, but I can't help it at the moment. The Universe will have to give me a pass on this sin. Basically, I'm just a kid in a crazy situation. How did I get into this, anyway? Oh, yeah, Arlene and her sneaky book and my deranged sister.

June is a Scorpio, as I said, and she can't imagine a situation that she couldn't sneak or sting her way out of.

There's a *USA Today* abandoned on a nearby table, so I snag it. I want to check our horoscopes.

Partly to irritate June, I read hers aloud: "Your theme for today is: Let go to move on. The Sun in determined Taurus forms several aspects in the midst of a life-changing Saturn-Pluto square. First the Sun squares expansive Jupiter, when misunderstandings can occur. Then the Sun trines independent Uranus to help you pull yourself up, if you keep your wits about you. Keep an eye on the Sun, though, as it squares Neptune next, and everything may not be as it seems. You are putting yourself out there on the line—is it really worth it? Find a way to protect yourself before you go into battle. Finally, Mercury's entrance into outspoken Sagittarius brings information you may or may not want to hear."

"Shut up, Cru." She takes a bite of her mega-hoagie and chews with her mouth open as she does when she's trying to gross me out. "Let me see the book."

I don't really want to bring it out in public, but I do. "Are your hands clean?"

She scowls, but she rubs them thoroughly with one of the wet-wipes the cafeteria thoughtfully provides in individual aluminum packets. She lays the book carefully on her knees, studying it absently for a moment.

Then she pulls out the ribbon and sealing wax. Why does she want to seal up the book? So I can't *see* things that she is not privy to, naturally. She doesn't know the book has a special affinity for me; I can *feel* how much it likes me. But I'm not going to try to stop her when she's on a roll. I'll figure out later how to get it open again when I need to.

"By parachute, bumbershoot, orris root—" She breaks off with a noise of frustration. "Give a hoot...." She trails off.

"Birthday suit?" I suggest, receiving in reply only a dirty look.

She taps the book three times and closes her eyes, her expression one of superiority (at least to me). She acts as if she has contacted a spirit and is dismissing it:

"By the winds let us part, leaving love in my heart. With these words of peace shall I break our connection. Peace be between us, and always great affection." Then she ties up the book with Girl Scout knots and great ceremony.

She's not particularly quiet. Nobody spares us a glance, though, not even the bored guy behind the grill. I suppose it's not that unusual for students to invoke the winds when they need to pass a meteorology exam.

June narrows her eyes at me. "I'm only giving this to you because you have a good hiding place for it in that zipper-filled pack, but I'll want it back in a bit. Stash it for me, please."

La-dee-dah. It's actually *my* book, but whatever.

I barely catch her toss, narrowly preventing the grimoire from landing in a puddle of semi-dried ketchup that somebody forgot to wipe off this table. It seems to appreciate that I treat it respectfully, or at least not as cavalierly as she does.

The book appears content to slide back into its hidey-hole. "We might need to unseal this soon," I mutter. There's no use arguing, so I let out a breath I didn't know I was holding and bus our table.

I put my hand on the outside of my backpack where I can feel the book, and from the vibes I can tell it's eager to get out. Silently I will it to be still. Her spell doesn't have any particular dominion over it, and it has an affinity for me. The shuddering quiets and my pack is quiescent. It heard me. Nyaah-nyaah, so there.

She's muttering something with her hands in the air like a Pentecostal during a charismatic worship service. "O Powers, help us believe in unseen realities. In this world that we help create, convince us there is something more than the material realm of atoms and synapses."

Of course there is. All matter is a wave until it's observed, anyway. Logic dictates that there must be a lot of waveforms we aren't currently observing or don't know how to observe yet. And string theory tells us of the other dimensions. She sounds like that TV preacher, Jack Osterizer. Who is she trying to pull a snow job on? Surely not the Powers.

Before I know I'm going to say it, I blurt out, "Why did I want to come with you?"

My sister slams her palms on the table. "I don't know why you came. Why don't you leave if you aren't going to help me? Do I have to do everything? Am I like the voiceover in one of those Adam Sandler movies? Do I have a name badge that says " 'Ask me to provide explanations'?"

"Yes," I say, knowing that she knows she's overreacting. I shouldn't have interrupted her prayer or whatever it was. "Sorry."

I hope we are not screwing up royally. Of course, as Gary always says, we learn so much more from our mistakes. I joke sometimes that I should be the most brilliant person ever, except maybe for Thomas Edison, who bragged that he knew nine hundred and ninety-nine ways *not* to make a light bulb. Lynwood says, "Sometimes mistakes stack up into awful situations that tear you apart, but if you can figure out how to put yourself back together again, you'll be so much stronger. Like a broken bone that mends."

June's typical reaction to that: "Horseshit."

I don't know who's right, but I do know I've got to hurry to catch up with my sister's long strides. She acts like she knows where she's going.

the lucky chapter

When we get back to the bus depot, we encounter a knot of giggling preteen girls inside, all carrying band instruments. I eavesdrop. It appears they are going to a music festival. Their private middle school is competing this evening in some kind of Guild contest at an arts conservatory in the suburbs. They need to arrive this afternoon in order to run through a few Sousa marches, evidently.

"This is it," June whispers. "The bus you saw."

I'm not sure. "Surely you jest."

"No, and don't call me Shirley," the two of us chorus in unison.

"Aren't we supposed to go to Chicago, not the sub-urbs here?"

"We have no way of knowing where he was actually headed," June says reasonably. A line is forming to board the local Greyhound. "We never saw his ticket. The book shows us a bus, we get on it."

I wish there had been a number on the bus the book showed me. "81" comes to mind, although I don't know why. It wasn't on the sketch.

"Come on." She steps into the boarding line.

Why not? We might pass as flugelhorn players. Or piccolo, in my case.

I can hardly keep from laughing as we queue up, be-cause this is like the scene in *Some Like It Hot*, but with-out Marilyn. The chaperones just wave us onboard with bored disinterest. They are counting heads, and I duck mine as I mount the bus steps. I'm hoping that having a couple of extras won't bug them too much.

Most of the girls have stored their instruments under the bus where the luggage goes, so we're not questioned as to where our John Philip Sousaphones might be. June manages to make conversation with a chaperone about playing brass. She's got a lot of brass herself: she likes to push it, see how far she can work a situation. Although I've seen her get away with so much, this still makes me nervous. I am trying to be invisible. Maybe some fumes remain from the earlier "Unnoticeable." I reach out to wrap them around me, but my astral fingers grasp dead air.

Some girl in front of us tosses her head, telling her seatmate, "Female drummers have to develop a hard shell, you know."

I wonder whether a hardshell drummer is anything like a hardshell Baptist? Not that I'd know, because I'm not musical. I'm not any good on my accordion (that was Gary's great idea.) I played the recorder for a while but took such heat from June about how dogs should be howling that I finally quit. The house wasn't big enough (even though it's huge) for me to get far enough away to practice without her having to endure my awful screeching tones.

I scoot over too close to June, apparently, because she shoves my pack that's sitting on the seat between us to the floor and replaces it with hers.

"Excu-u-use me," I say with exaggerated politeness.

She throws me that look I hate, the one that says, "Isn't it too bad that you like me more than I like you?"

I slump down in my seat. What was I supposed to do, salaam?

June's ring glitters in the sun. It catches my eye because she's wiggling her fingers like someone playing through an intermediate piano piece in her mind. It's kind of mesmerizing, and tearing my gaze away from it takes a bit of conscious effort. I blink a few times to dismiss the "sunspots" it leaves in my eyes.

June begins humming to herself: "Love For Sale." Having a Cole Porter moment here on the music bus, how picturesque. And some of the lyrics are so fitting for our situation.

Right now I'm also having pangs of conscience. The bus driver reminds me a little of Gary, or at least the back of his head does. That may not be so cool for him, because as I said, Gary looks like that guy who played the dad on that old Michael J. Fox sitcom *Family Ties* where Michael was Mr. Wind-Up Business Suit. Thinning gray hair at the temples, pointy chin covered with Van Dyke beard. The driver doesn't bear that close a resemblance, honestly. But it hits me hard, and I realize now that I miss home.

Both our parents are good people. Flaky, yes. Not completely in the real world, at least the one that I know. I must admit they are still Yuppies, though Yuppiedom is long over. But they also have endearing qualities. The lilt in Lynwood's voice…the way Gary's eyes crinkle when he smiles…the way they both lean into your conversation at the dinner table, as if nothing else matters more than your stupid anecdote in the here-and-now.

This attack of sentimentality might be Full Moon Fever. Wonder what phase the moon is in?

I unzip my pack absently and the book practically pops up out of it like a toaster pastry. Poking it back inside proves difficult. My sister glances over and hisses at me. "Stupid! Stop that."

"I'm not doing it on purpose. I was looking for—" What had I been looking for? I can't remember. "Gum." I do need gum or something to slake my sudden thirst, preferably a Diet Jolt Cola.

"You can't open the book now. I did a spell *binding*, airhead. It's bound."

Yet the book pops forth and unfurls its ribbons for me. It wants to talk to ME. I don't want to upset her and I have to live with her so I don't say anything. I just grab the ribbons and tie them back, giving the grimoire a couple of tentative pats as if to say, *wait until we're alone.* It sure is tempting to ask its advice again, because we're punting on a muddy field in a heavy rain.

"I wish you had *stayed* home." My sister's tone is dangerous. "Just try to be cool. Can you at least do that?"

My backpack is thudding. The grimoire is trying to get out. I reach in and push gently on the top of the book so it stays inside the backpack, hidden at least partially. I whisper to it, "Patience."

Still, I know I need help. I need a glimpse into what we've gotten ourselves into, because I have no idea what consequences our choices will bring. It's not something June will be thinking about, but I'm not sure any more. We should've let someone know where we are. We still could, but I know it would mean immediate capture as runaways, and goodbye to any chance of rescuing Arlene. The grown-ups would say she's made her own bed and should be left to her doom, I'm certain.

I don't know if we are doing the right thing.

What Would Justin Do? That game helps me not at all. Because I have no idea what my secret crush would do. Most of what I know about him I've constructed in my mind, and that isn't enough. *What Would Lynwood and Gary Do?* I cringe at the very idea of all that shouting.

The only place I have to turn is to an enchanted tome that I'm not sure I can trust. Even I can see how ironic that is.

Right now I can't look at the book, of course, not in front of all these people. I thrust it back down into the hidden compartment and zip my pack firmly.

June has her laptop open and is browsing the page called "Laws of Magic." Okay, "laws" are something she's never had much regard for unless she was bringing one down on someone else's head. But I hope she'll take these seriously.

My sister is a quick study. If she learns what she needs to know, I suppose she might not bring about Armageddon. Though I also realize that whatever she's involved in won't be an entirely benign procedure.

Peering over June's shoulder (but trying to keep my distance, meaning not touching her at any point), I read:

o. The Zeroth Law Of Magic is complex, but can be summed up as "plausible deniability": it can never be "provable" to the world at large that the ordinary laws of nature have been violated. Like other magical and natural laws, this is self-enforcing. Should one attempt to circumvent it, something else will give way instead.

Resulting, naturally, in disaster. A situation that you can't necessarily clean up. I'm getting the drift.

1. The First Law of Magic may be restated as "what goes around comes around": whatever you send to others will return to you threefold. This is commonly known as the Threefold Law.

I've seen enough. I get it. It's like the horriblescope
said: we're putting our own butts on the line. We've got
to protect ourselves, though I don't know how.

"I think that clerk would've helped us. I wish we had
let her." I'm talking about the shop owner, of course, but
too late I realize I'm not being clear.

"Shut up, Cruelest. Just shut it. I don't want to hear
you talk." June slams the laptop and scowls at me as if I
have been spying on her while she scribbled in her diary.
Little does she know. But I turn my head serenely to
stare out the window at the passing downtown.

Bars on most windows and concertina wire on building roofs tell me that this part of town is well-protected,
at least. A lot of places look closed, or at least the windows are boarded up.

Suddenly the bus decelerates strongly, throwing everyone back against their seats. The driver's good, because ten
cars ahead in the number two lane, a guy in a brand-new
cherry-red Honda has stalled and traffic is at a standstill.

Everyone's muttering. For some reason I glance back
and a couple of rows behind us, surrounded by girls, is a
lone man. He captures my attention because he's twen-
tyish (older than the band members, but not chaper-
one-like in the least) and strangely dressed. Wearing a
Washington University hoodie with the hood pulled up
around his face by its drawstring (making him look a bit
like that Jason character in the *Friday the Thirteenth* flicks
that I secretly viewed from the top of the stairs that time
June was allowed to watch the marathon on the movie

channel), and over that is a dark sweatshirt with the same university logo.

It's not that weird for him to be flying Washington University colors, as a few of the girls are wearing similarly-logoed items. And even though it's odd to wear a sweatshirt over a hoodie, I suppose the extra layer makes sense, because it's chilly in the bus, even out of the May wind. His Chicago Cubs cap is pulled down over the hood so the bill covers his face, and he wears sunglasses. I wonder how he even sees to get around.

Obviously I can't get a good look at him, but that nose is familiar. And his general demeanor, in fact...he sure is a lot like...*no, he can't be.* That's just guilt over our not rushing to find help for the Dark One or whoever he really was, although there's not much help for a guy with no flesh on his bones—and it's too gross to think about. I know this isn't him.

The bus swerves into the left lane to avoid the aftermath of a fender-bender. As we pull past the wreckage (with four people standing around variously waving their fists and crying), a few girls titter and a few scream.

"Nice driving," comes the cry from the peanut gallery in the rear seats.

We swing back into that lane and the bus totally sways, which grabs my attention back from the passengers as I grip the armrests. As if that's going to do me any good if we roll.

I glance over at June and it's like she didn't even notice the wreck. She's staring at her ring and how it glimmers in the sun. Probably thinking of Arlene and contemplating our next move. I can hope, can't I?

We hiss to a stop as a traffic jam halts the bus at a large intersection. June stirs and pats her backpack, apparently in search of something. I fetch my water bottle out of my bag as she pulls out her binoculars to scan the area.

"There," she crows, an outstretched finger pointing at something by the side of the road.

"What?"

"Can't you see?"

I put my finger to my lips to suggest an "inside" voice. "See what?"

June snorts her exasperation. Then she realizes she might've been a tad loud and crouches down towards me. "Look at the sign behind that building. The billboard."

She thrusts the binoculars into my hands. I hold the cylinders up to my eyes and focus. To no avail. All I see is a magnified insect that's stuck to the bus window. "I see your logic. Perhaps a giant mutant fly will give us a ride."

"Huh?" She snatches the looky-glasses back. "I forgot you can't read."

I strain my eyes in that direction, binoculars-free. Then I see it.

But I can't believe what I'm seeing. On a large billboard, left side is a photo of Arlene, smiling, caressing a bottled soft drink labeled HEX. With a caption next to her: "HERE I AM. YOU'VE FOUND ME!"

"It can't be," I begin, as the bus jerks forward with the traffic. We're moving again, and I lose sight of the sign as it fades into the rear view. Twisting in vain, I stare wildly at the back of the sign as it retreats. "That wasn't her. It's some kind of promo dealie with someone who looks like her."

But my tone of voice doesn't even convince me.

"She's here," June whispers, mostly to herself. "When we get off the bus, something will lead us to her."

"That would be nice. But let's not get ahead of ourselves."

"You're a downer. You're a detriment to me. I think we should split up." June turns her back.

It's just one of her moods. I hope.

Car horns blare behind us as the bus swerves again. Doesn't the driving bother anybody else? We don't seem to have squashed any bicyclists, so I suppose it's all right.

Something moves me to glance back at that lurker in the cap and hoodie, the one who has a nose so much like Arlene's dead boyfriend. He isn't looking at us. He's probably a secondary band teacher or a chaperone, after all. I am getting completely paranoid. And with good reason, I think.

The band director turns around to shout a few last-minute instructions, but she can't make herself heard over the murmur of the crowd. She shrugs and puts her headphones back into place. Meanwhile, one of the girls in front of us turns around as if she knows us and starts telling this long drawn-out joke, waving her arms and making faces. As if she's telling it to June because she requested it. Doesn't this chick realize that we're not part of her band?

Maybe June's spell, one of her spells, worked somehow and we're anonymous. Blending into the crowd.

The chick is holding a large oatmeal cookie and in mid-spiel takes a bite. Spitting crumbs, she continues her incoherent act-it-out thing. She's like one of those redneck comedians, one with no talent. The whole deal, with facial expressions and different voices for different characters and all. It reminds me of Gary's dumb shaggy-dog stories that are verses and verses long but go nowhere except to end on a stupid pun like "the sons of the squaw on the hippopotamus." Gary's much better at it, in fact.

My mind wanders (and no wonder) and I zone out. As usual, it drifts into a sea of numbers. I meditate on the various special properties of the Fibonacci numbers. Wonder whether 6495 has more than three factors? There's five and three, with 433 left over. Aha, 433 is prime. And so is 43, oddly enough. I sink into a calculating reverie. Before I know it, someone's shouting. "Take Highland. Left on Highland."

"Sunset," someone else cries from up front. "Turn on Sunset. There's mondo traffic on Highland."

The driver ignores them both and takes the next corner on two wheels (it feels like), screeching to a stop in front of a large elegant Midcentury Modern building that announces in cool neon that it is the Arts Conservatory of the Gateway Arch. We're apparently still in the St. Louis area, just not on the side of town where we started out.

Everyone immediately leaps out of their seats and crowds into the aisle. Not wanting to appear conspicuous, we insert ourselves into the closest gaps, and I end up separated from June by five or six girls. Six degrees of separation, as they say.

As soon as we get onto the wide steps leading up to the conservatory, I turn to find June. She's making good on her threat to split up, moving quickly away from me and up the steps. I notice the Cubs fan is also pushing his way over there.

Between us a throng of girls with tubas has materialized. I have no idea how they got them out from under the bus so quickly. One of them drops a huge black case practically on my feet and stops short in front of me. I rise to my tiptoes, but can only get glimpses of June. I'm starting to panic.

But then I see June standing still, looking up at the cool neon sign on the brick wall. I'm stuck in the middle of the chatty, pushing crowd. Violating all of Lynwood's rules about being a polite Southern lady, I begin shoving and squeezing through the crowd, ignoring the cries of, "Hey, watch it," and "Get back in line!" Nothing matters but getting up the steps to June.

I'm almost over to her when he reaches her first.

The hoodie guy is standing right next to my sister. As I watch helplessly, he reaches for her arm. Clawing my way up a few more steps, I get jostled from behind and almost trip. I grasp at people's uniforms to keep from hitting the pavement, heedless of the cussings I'm taking, and get myself back upright as soon as I can.

When I look again, June and the hoodie guy are gone.

I shriek, but the girls think I'm excited because we're here at last. They immediately start up one of those "Woo-hoo" cheers with fists pumping, and go into formation. Just like the sudden break into a song-and-dance in some ancient movie musical, plus everyone squishes up around me, and within seconds—exactly the way they say it happens when a child disappears and is kidnapped—the hoodie freak and June have disappeared completely out of sight.

Just like that.

free falling

I push through the crowd of girls, frantic. No sign of them. How could they get away so fast?

Bumping into and shoving aside the band members one by one, I run to the top of the conservatory steps and peer out over the street. Traffic in all directions—a million cars, taxis, buses. It's really cold, even though the breeze has died down. Suddenly the noise of the crowd, the sounds coming off the street, even the exhaust-stink of the city is debilitating. My chest is squeezed hollow, the blood rushing to my ears.

I pound down the street in the direction I thought I saw him looking. I'm running so hard my feet are throbbing…but I'm not even sure I'm going the right way.

Skidding to a stop at the corner, I pirouette and swivel my head in panic. There are cars and taxis everyplace and I know they could have climbed into any one of them.

I'm so screwed.

Dammit, that was him. The hoodie guy. And, if my instincts are correct, the same as Asmodeus, the Dark One.

Whoever.

My guts twist because my very being knows it's true. It must be some major magic he's using, to make it back from bone-land and take control like this. That dumb girl telling the long story was probably one of his conjure tricks.

I've been played like a fiddle at a bluegrass contest. Why, I don't know. It's all stupid. Especially me. And now…I'm pissed.

I reach into the pack and grab my GPS, but then I realize a GPS would be of no use. I don't know where they were going, and I have no address to give it. It doesn't matter where I am.

There's something else in my pack that could be of use. I still have the book.

I wander mindlessly through crowded sidewalks until I find a pocket park. There's a large tree beside a lamppost, and I sink down among its tangled roots, not caring that my butt is going to be caked with mud. I take comfort for a moment in the shelter of the leaves, the familiarity of the rough bark, and the faint odors of grass and earth.

Overhead, grackles claim the trees with loud caws. I can't help imagining they are laughing at me.

It's time to consult the tome.

Question is, is it my friend? Maybe the bad guys have been using it to track us all along. If I open it up, that may be just what they want. There could be a way of tracking its power. For all I know it is spying on us, a double agent. Is it a friend or my worst enemy?

I think back on how the book showed us this particular bus, perhaps setting up the snatch. So it does sort of seem as if the tome's an enemy. But perhaps the book's magic can also be fooled, so that it can be deceived about motives (in other words, it's not perfect.) Could be that the poor book has been conned, just as we have. Can it figure that out and counter the lies? Will it? Can I rely on it now?

I really don't have a barrelful of choices.

As I open the cover, the pages ripple. The book flips to the center page, seemingly sympathetic. And it apparently knows of my plight.

I could be imagining that.

No, it has something to show me. Pictures form. It runs through a series of black-and-white sketches. The cartoon panels roll past as if it's a flip book where someone has doodled on the edges of the pages, but I'm not having to flip; the scenes are simply going by.

The animation congeals into a movie. I see the Dark One, Asmodeus, dragging June by her upper arm down a maze of busy side streets—the names of which I cannot read—and stuffing her into a large sedan. Black, with tinted windows that must be just barely street legal, maybe a Lincoln or Caddy. As the car roars away, with my sister sprawled in the back seat appearing stunned, he berates her. (Too bad there's no sound.) She doesn't answer back, but looks glassy-eyed. She's having some kind of delayed reaction, because I know she's smarter than this; she always fights back. She scraps like a tomcat. So what's going on?

The silver ring glitters. June seems to come alert, blinking three times and licking her lips. She points her finger at him and her mouth flaps for a minute. I think she's trying to cast a spell like Sabrina Spellman on TV, but I also know June's magic finger doesn't work as well as any fictional comic book character's.

Sure enough, the blackguard merely laughs. He grabs her hand and yanks at the ring, but with no success. Now she's wailing and flailing at the door but there's no door handle inside, like in a police cruiser. For some reason I can't even see the back of the driver's head.

He reaches into his pocket and answers a cell phone. "WE HAVE APRIL," says a speech balloon. What? They have *June*.

Can't they tell us apart?

June is now fighting like an ocelot trying to rescue her litter. The jackass snaps the phone closed, grips her upper arms, and shakes her. Tears spill down her cheeks.

I can't watch. No, I have to look. I don't know what I missed while my eyes were closed, but when I reopen them, the car has parked. He leaps out and tries to pull

her along, but she goes limp and hangs on to the up-
holstery, so he slaps her. The driver takes her feet (I still
can't see a face) as the kidnapper gets her under the arms,
and they carry her inside a huge brick building. I can't
read any signage or see anything about the place.

The show stops and the page goes blank.

"You are downright mean," I tell it. "This was just a
tease. Show me which way to go. A map would be easy
enough."

The book is blank and still. A dead weight.

I'm trying to think, but nothing happens.

This is hopeless. June needs me and I am failing her
once again.

Overhead, the birds, oblivious to my pounding heart,
chirp merrily away.

I'm going to be sick. At least my adrenaline response
is working properly, because I am full of go-power and
ready to fly through the air like a Powerpuff girl...if
only I knew in which direction to wing it. Hormones
are pouring out of all my ducts like an internal scream.

Okay, I can do this. I'm going to try to cast a spell. The
heck with protocol. If I humble myself before the powers,
perhaps they'll take pity on me.

The book lies open on my knees, blank as a new ream
of twenty-pound printer paper.

"O Hidden Powers, ye ones of great ability. Take pity
on me, a stupid mortal girl," I begin in a wobbly voice. I
have no confidence at all that I'm being heard. "O Powers, I must find my sister. She is a blameless innocent
and has done nothing to come to your hostile attention."

(June, a blameless innocent like some kind of puppy? No way, but I'm going for sympathy here.) "She deserves your powerful assistance. Help me rescue her."

Passersby are shooting me funny looks. I smile gamely, as if I am merely rehearsing for a play (that was the excuse Sabrina Spellman used to use all the time) or reciting a poem for school. "O Powers of Great Import," I add, for good measure.

The strains of that forgotten tune reach me again. The one Gary was whistling, the one I heard in my mind's ear. I don't know where the music is coming from. But I suddenly remember Gary naming that tune.

It's "I Remember April," a jazz standard. This must be a good sign that the Powers are listening and they remember me.

"More cowbell," I say in a fit of whimsy. I hear bells now in the music. It's like the ethereal bell I heard, or imagined I did, when I cast the first spell, the cantrip that worked.

So I keep talking. "Okay, let's see what we can do when we don't know what we're doing. I mean, when I don't know. I'm aware that YOU know perfectly well."

I am such a lamer at small talk with magical grimoires.

I get the feeling I need to make some kind of gesture. There are those material components left from June's attempts, the feather and the incense and so forth. And I consider the concept of a material sacrifice. (It's not that different from chemistry experiments, in which you sacrifice the baking soda to the vinegar, for example.) I lay this stuff out in a tarot-card sort of arrangement, but I'm not getting a special feeling from any of it. Where's the nearest voodoo priestess when you need her?

"Help me, please," I say quietly, taking the book back on my lap.

The book flashes a picture in the top right-hand corner. It's like some kind of chat window. The "helpful paperclip," if you will. It's showing a lucky charm. Not as in the cereal, ha ha, but like a rabbit's foot. Although that can't have been lucky for the rabbit.

I'm guessing what it wants. I need a talisman.

Somehow I know it instinctively. What would be important enough? Perhaps something of my grandmother's, although not the New Testament this time. Digging my grandmother's thimble out of the sewing kit in my bag where I have it as a sentimental keepsake, I fix it on the thumb of my left hand.

The book must approve, as it's now displaying a happy-face symbol in that "window." Good thing this entity has a help mode.

I use the thimble to trace the symbol—a rune?—on the page and in the air. "O Powers," I begin. "Take pity on me, a sinner and an idiot who needs help."

I smell gardenias in the rain. Lynwood has a huge bush out back that we get cuttings from all summer. The page in the book turns a heavenly sky blue around the green tracing of the rune. Any moment I might hear it booming out, "Zül!"

My thumb burns. The thimble glows magenta.

Then it's gone.

I suppress a yelp. If I had known the book planned to TAKE the talisman, I would've used something else that I didn't mind sacrificing. "That's not fair!" I can't help myself. A couple more people on the sidewalk glance over at me, and I force another innocent smile as I wave the guilty hand.

After my hammering heart quiets down, I shed a few tears and decide to put on my grown-up panties. June needs the thimble (or the sacrifice it represents) more than I do at the moment. I would've eventually lost the thimble carrying it around like that, anyway.

On my lap now is the shimmering feather. Did it fall out of the backpack? I can't remember taking it out. But there it is now. Which must mean that I need to use it next.

I grasp the feather with my other hand. (The book could've taken that instead, easily. But then it isn't supposed to be easy, is it?) So what do I do with it? I wave the feather in hypnotic circles. "I beseech thee, help me." Then I trace a question mark in the air. "Take me where I am supposed to go to rescue my sister."

In inky letters comes the answer.

First ye must be protected from harm.
Repeat after me.

I almost giggle. What a clichéd catchphrase, right out of the old movies I love. But I sober up instantly, because I agree. I definitely need a sword and a shield, like the people in June's sorcery novels.

Lucky thing the foot traffic around here has fallen off. Nobody's here to stare at me, for the moment. I picture myself in an isolated grove of trees in a friendly forest. Visualizing rings of purple and gold around me can't hurt.

The ink begins flowing again.

"By the dragons' light I call to thee,

Diana's fair moon, ruler of the night."

(I dutifully incant this, even though it's not quite dark yet.)

"I call to thee by the powers of three—"

(—a math spell, right up my alley).

"I conjure thee to protect me with thy might,

From all wicked spirits and any enemy.

Thrice around the circle bound,

Sink all evil to the ground.

So must it be!"

My voice cracks, but I manage to get it all said.

Now are you charged with your mission.

Walk to closest intersection.

Head due north until it's time to turn.

The sun is beginning to sink lower. Soon it will be early dusk, and I don't want to wander in the dark. I hope I will know where to turn. Presumably something will tell me.

I hope.

I am feeling kind of floaty, partly from almost no sleep and partly because this has to be a bad dream. But my feet and legs say otherwise. According to them (and my newest blisters), I've trekked blocks and blocks. Across town, practically. Into a district of empty warehouses and abandoned stores with boarded-up windows. A few dive bars seem to be in operation, but I wouldn't want to have to seek help from that quarter.

The damp air pierces my clothing, and I shiver. It's too cold for early spring. Or maybe I'm terrified. I'm having a spell of nervous rigors, as Southern belles say when they're in withdrawal from mint juleps. I pull on my hoodie and lace the strings so I'll be more anonymous. Like the perp.

Then I visor my hand and scan the horizon in hope of some kind of clue, to get oriented.

I'm looking, waiting, watching for a sign. What kind of sign? Where to turn, obviously, but there has been nothing. Signs are for giving direction, for pointing out a way. To where?

Weary and road-bored, I begin walking again, using the GPS to verify true north. I've trudged several more blocks when a bell rings inside my head, a silver chime like a Christmas peal from a church steeple. I know it means this is the place.

I stop and try to be alert, vigilant, whatever. By standing stock-still and listening for the vibrations of the universe. The only sound is my own breath slipping out.

Across the street, I catch a glimpse of movement. Judging by the clothing and general outline, it's him. The hoodie guy from the bus. He's a dead (ha ha) ringer for the Dark One.

He slips around the corner. I take off after him.

We pound down the short industrial blocks. It's increasingly isolated and I have a sense of foreboding. The area is also kind of seedy, so I keep glancing around to make sure I'm not flinging myself headlong into a gang's turf. In the blurry twilight, I think I see him dodge down an alley.

That freezes me in place. I'm not about to follow him into an obvious trap. The loitering few on the street eye me warily as I stand there like Henny Penny.

In a moment his face reappears, peering around the corner at me. He raises his arm and I can't hear the word he mutters, but something flashes in his hand. What is that ball of blue light?

He makes a throwing motion. The streak of light is coming straight for me. Faster than I can get out of the way.

I see stars. My visual field becomes all star-field and then goes stark white, even though I am fighting for consciousness. As I fight against the abyss, I feel myself falling backward.

When I open my eyes, I'm flat on my back on the side-walk with three of the slackers who had been leaning up against the cold brick walls gathered around me. They smell like weed and sweat, but they're beautiful to me right now.

"What happened?" I push up on my elbows and a so-licitous Good Samaritan pushes me back down. He wears a torn tracksuit and his face is surrounded by shiny black braids like licorice whips.

"You like passed out or something," he says in wonder. "Maybe you better take it easy."

"Did you see that bright light hit me?"

He shakes his dreadlocks. "Nothing happened to you. Your eyes like just rolled back in your head and you fell on me and my buddy. Good thing we were there to lower you to the pavement or you'd like be bruised all over. You didn't hit your punkin head. Thank my buddy Josh for that."

"Thank you all." I'm fairly sore, but my butt only stings and hasn't started really smarting yet. I struggle to my feet with the Samaritan's help. "Thank you so much." My clothes are rumpled and torn, but that's the cur-rently edgy style, anyway.

Another reluctant rescuer holds up my pack, which I'd nearly forgotten about.

The Samaritan explains. "My buddy saved your back-pack just as some lowlife was about to make off with it.

Actually, it was like on the ground and the stealing dude had his hands on it, but when Josh lunged over there, it like leaped into his arms from the ground and the thief scuttled."

The book! I nod and thank them profusely. A quick palpation of my pack reassures me that the book is there, its heft and temperature (for some reason it's heated up a bit, perhaps from my body?) a comfort in the secret compartment.

"You weren't out but a sec," offers Josh. "You feel better?"

"I'm really all right now." They look at me worriedly. Anne Frank was right—people are still mostly good inside, when it counts. Most people, anyway.

The third slacker, a skinny girl standing behind the two men, looks fairly spaced out, but is still sharp enough to ask, "Shouldn't we call an ambulance? You, like, might need to be checked out for a concussion or broken bones."

"I appreciate your concern, but nothing important banged against the pavement." I rub my butt without thinking, because that part did hit the concrete, but it's only insulted and not damaged.

"Wow, like, it didn't, I'm sure," said my erstwhile rescuer. "Like we caught you just as you went limp and went down. Weirdest thing I've ever seen."

The protection spell. I guess it must be working.

"I'm, like, fine now." His patois is contagious. I manage to get balanced on my feet and re-shoulder my pack, though I wince when it hits my right shoulder. I wiggle it back into its primary position. "You're good people. I'm okay thanks to your help. Go in peace."

They eye me warily again and watch me for a short time, then wander away, leaving me to investigate that alley. Surely that's what I'm supposed to do?

When I got clocked by the blue light ball, the Hoodie Guy expected me to be unconscious out here for a long time, perhaps even taken away to a hospital, I'll bet. Thus, he and whoever's helping him are not expecting me. This is the time to move.

The alleyway is a dead end, just a dumpster and then a blank wall. I despair. Wandering back out to the now-deserted street, I look up at the dilapidated old building on the closest corner.

It looks somehow familiar.

cosmodemonic

The sun has faded the surface around where the old sign was. Examining the shadow-letters, I make an educated guess as to what this is.

It's the abandoned Cosmodemonic Telecom building. They were "the other phone company" at the turn of the century. So old that they started out in the days of the telegraph. But out of business now, overtaken by technology. I read about this place in one of Lynwood's old architecture books, because it was once a grand old dame of a building. And like I said, I don't forget much of anything.

Anyhow, St. Louis is an old town. Famous architect or not, this is basically a hundred-year-old factory warehouse. Blue front door with most of the paint scrubbed off, broken windowpanes here and there, two stories with the inside mostly empty downstairs. The wide curving staircase going up from the middle of the bottom floor is completely trashed, most of the treads missing or half-hanging off the metal substructure. This looks like a carnival funhouse filled with discarded dreams and maybe a few ghosts.

Behind the other downstairs windows I see only stacks of old cartons and boxes that I imagine are home to endless mice and a few bats. Upstairs, though, there's a light from a window.

I hear that music again. "I Remember April."

"All right, already," I tell the Powers. "I like the tune as well as the next person." My voice echoes through the shadows. "Message received loud and clear." Although I still don't know what I'm supposed to do.

Climb the wall?

Not that I'm good at it, but I have done some climbing. I imagine that I am on the climbing wall at Indoor Canyons at home as I try to place my hands. I can't climb with my pack on my back (try it sometime), so I reluctantly drop it among the rubble and start up.

The bricks are those old long and wide 1950s Frank Lloyd Wright jobbies, and they're irregularly set so it looks as if I can get footholds. Slowly I inch along the wall, but it's exhausting. I clamp myself against the wall like a barnacle on a scow in Davy Jones' Locker and rest my left cheek on the bricks, trying to think.

All the slackers who helped me have cleared out. The street is absolutely abandoned. I could really use a hook-and-ladder with those extra rungs just about now. I scan the structure again, looking for anything to help me.

At the corner of the building, there's a rusted old fire escape and a landing that goes across half the wall. Including a narrow stretch that reaches almost under that window. Duh! I was trying to think, but I only had to look.

The fire escape ladder starts about eight feet up, but underneath it is the shell of a dumpster. I shudder to think what might live inside that old metal. Don't want to fall in there and get trapped. Shut up, caged heart—you're not a bird. I can't push the behemoth closer, but I'll bet I can just barely grab onto the ladder from its edge.

I tighten the straps of my backpack and make the jump to the side of the dumpster. Shinnying up without getting cut by a rusty edge is pretty tough, but I manage to get on the top without tipping the thing over (sometimes being a little bitty mite is a Good Thing) and make my way to the side where the fire escape ladder hangs.

The metal groans and creaks as I grab on and pull myself up. I hope it isn't loud enough for anyone inside to hear. Maybe they'll attribute any noise to the wind. Or maybe no one is in here at all, and I'm on a wild-goose chase, with my sister the silly goose.

I make it to the end of the fire escape, just short of the window, before I have to take a rest. I'm considering shimmying horizontally along the widest part of the ledge in order to get a peek inside when footsteps thump into that room, and I duck back instinctively, even though I couldn't have been seen from where I was. I flatten myself against the gridded metal anyway.

Muffled voices leak through the broken panes.

"She's not very alert yet," someone says. "You gave her too much of the stuff."

"No, this is normal," says another voice.

"It's fine," snaps another voice, a raspy sound that turns my chest to ice. "She doesn't have to be on the ball, as long as she's on the cot."

It can't be.

A familiar cackle confirms my worst fear.

That's Arlene.

I start to tremble all over. Even my toes cramp inside my ill-fitting footwear. My stomach clenches and I fight the urge to hurl. Can this be real? Could my favorite cousin who's my mother's special pet have betrayed us?

Arlene's big entrance as Master of the Wicked Ones sucker-punches me. I can't deny that I perceive what I perceive, impossible as it is. She is not their prisoner, but their leader.

A tear or two escapes before I "man up" (as Gary often says when he means to encourage us—note the word "courage" in the middle of the word—to be brave). I suck in a breath but suppress a sob, because this is not the time to be a sissy. I have to be tough.

I've got to risk looking inside.

The top of my head is hooded in black from my sweatshirt, so if my face isn't glowing with fear, maybe they won't notice me. I slide upward just enough to peer in.

June is in a bare room on a metal cot. She's cuffed to the headboard's metal uprights, which I know would be making her crazy if she were awake, because she can't stand to have her hands held above her head, let alone confined. There's a pole lamp casting circular light on the ceiling overhead, but the room is fairly well lighted by the first rays of sunset, warm light streaming in through the window. Across from her there's a wide-open area with a platform like a pulpit and large rocks that form a semi-circular wall around the platform. The "stage" floor is mainly cleared, as if they've gathered in there recently. To stand around, to hear a lecture, to— what? There are two acolytes at her side, probably the people I heard arguing.

Arlene stands at the door, looking angry. "You idiots. You snatched the wrong one." She waves her arms as though calling a cheer for good old Wilson Junior High.

"What?" says one of the clueless.

Her hands fly to her hips. "This is not April."

"You said the plain one." He blinks.

"They're *both* plain," adds the other guy in a reasonable tone. "The one with the ugly hair, you said. This one fits the bill."

Arlene takes a step into the room, rolling her head on its stalky neck as if to relieve a crick. "No-o-o-o." She makes a snorty sound of disbelief and then sucks in a loud breath, as though she's thinking. "But we'll punt. We have her, we can take something."

Apparently she really is the group's leader—duh—because the two scruffy young men follow her as she paces back and forth. Now that she's not blocking the doorway, I can see several more people lurking in the opening. How many are there?

She snaps her fingers. "I know. She has this way of sneaking up on people. The Ninja power. That's got to be marketable."

"She registers zero on the magic scale. Are you sure it's there?"

Arlene's eyes look ceilingward, as if imploring the Evil Powers to give her patience. "Take whatever. Whatever you think is useful." She throws her hands into the air. "I can't watch. You do it."

"I've got to set up. And I'll need three people."

"Take care of it. And don't screw this up." Arlene flounces out.

She can't watch? At least she retains some semblance of feeling for June. Or maybe she just finds these magical moments boring. More likely, she doesn't want to have the Rule of Threefold Returns invoked on her for the spell.

The others follow. Apparently, since June's out and cuffed, it's no problem leaving her momentarily alone.

Though I have the feeling they'll be back quite soon.

How could Arlene do this? More to the point, why would she? My breath catches in my throat as I begin to realize that Arlene's visit to our house was more than a simple escape route from her parents. She wanted something from June…no, actually, from me. But what could it be? What do I have that Arlene couldn't buy with her drug money, or steal from somebody else? And how did Arlene know for sure that we'd follow her? How did she know we'd find her?

Well, that part's easy. The ring and the book, of course.

Did the book bring me here to rescue June, or to gloat over how easily the old switcheroo was pulled on dumb little us?

Or is this all just a misunderstanding?

Come on, not even June could rationalize it as *that.* Or Lynwood with her perpetually cheery outlook and her refusal to see the dark side of things. No, this was deliberate. We were snookered, as someone's billiards-playing grandfather surely still says.

I still don't classify Arlene as "evil." Her actions are evil, but she's not that nice. She's wicked. There's a difference.

As I watch my sister, a movement catches my attention.

June blinks.

Did I just SEE that?

Yes! Her eyelids flutter open. She's awake! Or at least no longer unconscious.

Her gaze darts over to the window. The light suddenly comes on in her eyes and I make the shushing motion. One of the bad guys could be lurking just beyond the doorway, and I don't want anyone to hear. Did I make a noise to attract her attention? If so, I hope she was the only one who heard.

Thank God she's not down for the count. Has she been playing possum? The thought that she might've been makes me feel so much better. In a sense, anyway.

To be sure she understands, I make the ASL sign for "shut up," which is where you grab your lips and press them together like a duck's bill.

She blinks twice, but this time I think it's with conscious intent.

"Play dead," I mouth. And just in time, as those two troop back in holding various items that I assume are paraphernalia for...for...whatever they're going to do.

I watch for a few seconds, and then I feel something wet on my cheek. Dashing away the tears (which did not have permission to exit), I tuck myself back down beneath the windowsill to think. Like Arlene, I can't watch.

One of the jerks says, "Her Highness gave her too much. She'll be out for hours."

"Girl didn't know what hit her." The second voice sounds mildly sympathetic.

"Well, all the better for us." Noises of searching through a basket commence. "Bloody Hepzibah! I don't have all the components. Come on, help me find the serum. It's got to be with the other stuff."

"You should've made sure it was in with this stuff before we came back. If she catches us, she'll be all in our faces about being inefficient."

"You were the one loading the basket. You should've checked." A pause. "Did she just blink?"

"No! It's your imagination. Like I said, she's down for the count."

"She'd better be. We've got to round up the others and get this done. It's going to take a while to set up."

"Come on, then." Another pregnant pause. "I swear she just blinked at that window."

"She didn't! I was watching. Now, come on."

Lucky thing that this guy is the type of jerk who thinks he knows everything, and that the other one is a born follower. They argue in this vein, though, for a bit longer.

Squeezing my eyes closed, I will them to forget it and to go on. If June doesn't give me away. The moments stretch out like taffy as I wait to be betrayed. Evidently, she doesn't do anything suspicious, and they finish arguing and slam out the door.

The window is cracked open slightly at the bottom, probably for air. It's easy for me to slide my palms underneath the splintered wood and push it wide enough to crawl in. The squeal isn't all that loud, despite the rust on the sash.

While I slither through the opening, I'm making the shushing motion to June. Her eyelids are fluttering again. She seems groggy, as if coming out of anesthesia.

But she understands the essentialness of quiet. I can communicate with hand signals. That sign language and finger-spelling that Lynwood's so proud of is finally coming in handy. Handy, ha ha. Except that June's hands are captive, so she can't tell me anything important.

Of course what she'd probably say is, "Get me out of here!"

I'm not sure if I can lift my sister because she's so heavy. Then I notice that not only is she locked to the iron headboard with handcuffs, but also her feet are confined to the mattress by fairly heavy bonds. A hacksaw and blowtorch are not among my supplies, alas.

We don't know how soon they'll be back, and all we need is for me to be caught as well. Maybe these are excuses, but for now, she'll have to stay.

This bunch thinks they're so secret and special, I'll bet. Well, even if I can't do it from here, I can still watch them. And show the world what they are doing.

Because I've remembered the Bunny doll I have in my backpack, the one with the built-in broadcasting digital camera. Life is so ironic: June started out so contemptuous and declared it a toy.

Now that I'm inside, I see all sorts of junk in the room: old crates covered with dusty tarps, piles of broken planks, a stack of pizza boxes that still stink of onions and pepperoni. I spend a moment doing reconnaissance and find a place between some boxes in the corner where I can secrete Bunny. I set up the video doll where she won't be easily noticed, but where her lens has a clear view of June and can spy on the wicked ones. All I have to do is activate it remotely with my smartphone.

I slip back over to June. "I'll be back," I whisper furiously in her ear. On an impulse, I plant a light smooch on June's forehead.

It tells me just how crocked she still is that she doesn't rear back or flinch from the kiss.

I hate to climb back outside on that skinny ledge (it looks a lot more dangerous from inside here, looking down), but them's da breaks, pardner. In the gathering twilight, it's tough to see exactly where to put my feet, so I go partly by feel. When the window slides closed, this time it makes a SCHREEK noise like chalkboard fingernails. I wince.

Still, I don't hear any footsteps running to see what that noise was. Maybe they're all partly deaf. It would serve them right.

After waiting a few seconds to be sure there's no response, I scramble down to the metal landing. I've got to get help, and I know how to do it.

Of course the ideal thing would be to dial 911. But calling the police isn't an option for me right now. It's not just that I have been getting one-half bar, very poor reception, on the phone since I was on the bus. What would I say to the dispatcher, other than, "There's a bunch of slackers staying in an abandoned warehouse doing magic on helpless teenagers?" Sounds like a prank call or a kid trying to get others into trouble, and they'd never listen.

And as a wanted teen runaway (I assume there's been an Amber alert issued by now, knowing Lynwood), I could announce that I am ready to turn myself in—but then the cavalry would rush here with sirens screaming, tipping off the hoodlums and allowing them plenty of time to drag June to another hideout off who-knows-where while I wasted time trying to explain. They'd escape, and by the time we could find them again, they could have done something even more terrible to June.

I don't know how to make the authorities understand that June is not inside of her own free will and is actually in danger. Right now it only looks like some sort of Thespian initiation for bondage fans. I will call soon, but I'll have to consider what to say so they don't dismiss me as a crank.

Besides, I need this screen right now to monitor what's going on inside.

With my phone, I send the camera the "on" signal. Bunny's streaming the data to a webcam page that my smartphone can display with fairly quick buffering. Picture is pretty good, actually. Sound is a tad muffled, but not bad, if I could hear it over my heart pounding in my ears.

A couple of the loonies enter the room, waving their arms, holding something smoldering in each fist. I realize they're smudging the room (it's a spiritual thing with earth religions) with the smoke from a bundle of dried herbs and twigs. The scene is out of a B-movie, some bad horror flick from the 1970s starring failed has-beens. My sister lies on the cot, impassive, looking stoned out of her gourd.

I tell the page to capture this as a MP4 video so I can post it on YourTube and link it to a status update on my FaceThis account. And June's. And I'll also e-mail it to Lynwood and Gary and the police and Justin (just in case, Justin, ha ha), and someone's got to wake up and pay attention.

Still, it would be nice if I could prevent the ritual in the first place.

I can't run for help physically; I need to hunker down here nearby so that if they start hurting June, I can burst in and save her, like…like a ninety-six-pound weakling?

I can't think straight in this crooked place.

Not right now, anyway, because more hooded acolytes are gathering around the end of my sister's bed in a semicircle like a bunch of Tri-Delts about to swear in a newbie.

I watch on the smartphone, helplessly, as eleven ruffians crowd around my sister's cot. Three apparently didn't cut it, or else they all wanted to watch. Clad in black hoods like Ringwraiths out of Tolkien, accompanied by close-fitting black T-shirts and black leather pants, with black candles stuck into cored apples flickering in their grasps. They form a Circle and hold hands. Just like "Flying Dutchman" on the playground.

In full Goth makeup (hood-free) and a black maxi-dress with fringed sleeves lending witchy splendor, Arlene sweeps in. Attending the ritual, despite what she said, and completing (I surmise) the required Twelve for a coven. She doesn't look too regretful, either. She can barely suppress her grin as she steps into the front and the ring drops hands. Those cold, cold hands and cold hearts.

Two dunderheads step forward to lay a white sheet over my sister, leaving only the top third of her face exposed to the air. They all begin humming the same note in unison, which gets louder and louder. As their voices swell, the light in the room gets brighter. A black candle suddenly flares on a round plant stand set at the head of the bed. I either didn't see it before, or their magic lighted it.

At the foot of the bed they've placed a chair holding a basket of what looks like limes. Citrus fruit? Kinky.

When Arlene nods, one of the guys breaks circle and steps forward from behind her. He taps June on the forehead.

She opens her eyes and spits at him.

Man, are they ever surprised. I kind of am, too, because she seemed somewhat comatose there for a while. My sister has seen too many World War II movies and has apparently imprinted on Ingrid Bergman—who didn't get away with it, either.

Arlene steps over and pops June one in the kisser. And not gently, either. The head acolyte or whatever he is taps June's forehead again, hard, and she's perfectly still.

They pass a lime forward to Arlene, and I see that it's precut in two. She takes the two halves and places them on June's cheeks. (But not before slapping each cheek, and not so lightly.) Then she palms a stone out of one of her pockets and puts it on June's forehead. One of June's stolen amethysts, it looks like.

June knew better than to steal magical things.

My cousin is quite the drama queen, as if I hadn't known. She chants and keens and sings as she circles June's bed. Rubbing her long mean index fingers against her thumbs, she sprinkles some kind of powder on the candle flame that's on the stand, and the blue flame turns red. Then she waves her hands over her head in a snaky fashion, like a belly dancer in full swing.

I'm surprised Arlene doesn't wave a plucked chicken over her head for effect. They probably just used up their last one.

This is not a ritual of white witchcraft or anything you could call an earth-friendly religion, that much I can say for sure. They're meddling with things man was never supposed to get involved in.

My sister begins to glow. It's a weak lavender light emanating from her skin and illuminating her form beneath the covering sheet, as though she has swallowed a fluorescent tube. Could that be an aura?

A rumble like the sound of an earthquake overwhelms the phone's speaker, which cuts out, but the sound transmission comes back as that fades to a whistle.

A flash of dark purple light swirls around June. Then the light becomes a small genie-like funnel cloud and enters the stone. Those long fingers reach out, and the stone plops onto the fat palm of a laughing Arlene.

The ritual is over.

I slide the NetBook out of my pack and confirm that the video was captured at the site as well as being broadcast live. It's on the VideoDollies website, just the way

the owner's manual said it would be. Auto-magically
sent from Bunny and saved.

Bringing up the "views" list, I note that there have already been three surfers who've at least clicked on the
video. The total ramps up to seven…no, twenty-nine.
The numbers look good. This is going to work.

I've done it.

I can e-mail the video to Lynwood and Gary (though
they don't always understand how to open attachments,
and this is a huge video file that might be truncated by
our ISP), but for insurance I'll send it to Justin Fink as well.

First I post it on YourTube and link to our Face-
This pages as planned. Quickly I type a description in
the "what is this" field of the video, asking for our rescue.
In another window I e-mail Lynwood, Gary, and Justin
with a plea to watch the clip, and I also send the link
to the TweetyBird feed of our homeschooling bunch. I
give the street address of where we are and beg for immediate help.

However, most people are bound to think it's a prank.

In fact, I'm sure they do, as I don't hear any sirens yet.
I don't know how to send this directly to emergency
services, but as soon as I figure that out, I'll add a note
that they should come silently to have the advantage of
surprise.

To Justin I Tweet the GPS coordinates of where we
are. He'll be the only one who knows what the heck I
am sending when I give the waypoint. He's not online
live on Twitter right now, more's the pity. He'll pick it
up fairly soon.

Surely he will.

Law enforcement is my best hope. What could the witches be arrested for? Chanting over someone? They'll say we came here of our own free will. They'll say our cousin brought us willingly along. That it was just a fun hoax on us, or a practical joke. It's mainly trespassing. I've got to have more than this.

But I saw what was going on and I believe it worked. I know it did. That's the bad part.

This is what they do: They steal talents.

I surmise that what's now inside the amethyst is the essence of June's lost talent.

(They were after mine.)

Our darling Arlene (ever the expert at finding unsavory characters to hang with) discovered an easy way to make money using other people's gifts, aptitudes, and abilities. People with lots of cash but no morals come to this group and say, "I want to be able to do math," or sing, or draw, whatever. So they've found a magic way to give people these abilities. But where do the talents they bestow come from? Answer is that they cannot create them, for only God gives out talents, so they have to steal them from unsuspecting victims.

It's the worst kind of theft. It's stealing part of somebody's soul.

It's not just talents, but I'm calling it that for convenience. If someone has an extensive database or knowledge base about a topic, they strip that out, and afterwards there's a doctor on the street because he has forgotten anatomy and physiology and wanders the streets saying, "Hamstring? Or rudder?" He has it all confused with boats. And he doesn't know how he lost his knowledge.

This is all conjecture, of course, but I'm a good guesser.

It is time to make the phone call I've been dreading. The one I've been putting off. Even though we'll be punished (grounded for eternity, sent to a convent if they can find one with fifteen-foot walls, put into a military boot camp, I don't know what), I need to call Lynwood and get rescued. She'll send the police; it won't be thought to be a prank if it's an adult saying her minor daughters are in danger. I just keep procrastinating because I know there'll be shouting and she's going to be upset with us, and justifiably so.

Actually, it'll have to go by e-mail, because I still don't have the bandwidth for a phone call. Do I? On the smartphone, I check the antenna icon, and I've got three bars. Now I can close the NetBook and call Lynwood and maybe also the cops.

I'm about to dial. Really, I am.

But it's hypnotic watching the end of their ritual (likely some sort of thanks or tribute to the Dark Powers). The sound is still on, but it doesn't mean anything to me because it's not in any language that has been spoken in this world for a couple of thousand years. Seriously, it doesn't sound Indo-European, Anglo-Saxon, Celtic, or even Double Dutch; it strikes my ears like nothing people could make up.

My sister lies perfectly still, either passed out or playing possum—six of one, half a dozen of the other—and I'm worried. She had been awake enough to spit at them, but then they punched her, tapped her on the forehead, and slapped her a couple of times, and she hasn't twitched since. What if they've done something to her and she doesn't wake up? Or she wakes up and she's no longer…herself?

I am so busy watching the live feed that I don't hear somebody creeping up from behind. Before I can make a sound, I'm in someone's strong arms, my mouth and eyes covered by stinky hands with dirty fingers. It smells like rotten pork. Like the hoodie guy when he was all bones on the train.

Have I mentioned I'm screwed?

the april witch

I manage to stuff the smartphone down my bra
because it got slammed up against my chin when I was
grabbed. Maybe the minion of doom didn't notice.

Inside, the acolytes' hoods are thrown back and the
wicked faces look harmless, even slacker-ish. Shrieks
of surprise and pleasure ensue as I am dragged into the
room. Arlene is nowhere to be seen.

"The April Witch," says a dandelion-headed white
man derisively. "Thought she was going to play Wonder
Woman." He kicks at the leg of the cot. He stubs his
toe instead on a metal chair with a rotted-out fabric seat
and one short leg, and curses.

An older frizzy harridan gets in my face. She squeezes my upper arm, activating that perma-bruise that June created years ago. "I know about the April witch. You're possessed, and I'm going to take you out. Far out." She laughs. The term is from an old Ray Bradbury story that I did a report on in fifth grade for Gary. The April witch possesses a human girl so she can know love. But love is the furthest thing from this harridan's mind as she glares at me with demonic rays. "You stupid little witch."

"Takes one to know one," I gasp out. My smart mouth does not know when to shut up.

She slaps me across the face. It really smarts.

The dandelion guy grabs my NetBook, which I've apparently been clutching against my chest, and smashes it to the floor. He and the harridan dance the tarantella on it with their feet, breaking the hinge and shattering the screen. At least I had snapped it closed by reflex when I was snatched up, and my kidnapper didn't see what I was doing. Or isn't that computer-savvy. I'm sure it was finished sending everything that was queued up to be sent. Fairly sure.

The one holding me reaches around to snatch my cell phone out of my cleavage. I gasp, but he isn't there to grope, just to get the device. He hands it to the harridan, and as everyone watches, she stomps it to pieces. When the screen cracks, I can almost hear Gary's wallet screaming in pain.

He drops me on the floor from a couple of feet up, and now I see that it is, indeed, our trainswain, the Dark One. Hoodie Guy. Asmodeus. So we were fooled by an illusion back on the train. Or by some other kind of magic. Probably both.

"Now, my pretty," Harridan says in her best Wicked Witch voice, "as for you."

"Get back," says the dandelion head, shoving her away. "This one isn't yours. It belongs to the High Priestess personally."

They tie my arms and legs to the metal chair, dragging it to the foot of the cot. It's another scene straight out of every black-and-white horror flick that used to play at drive-ins. They're not paying attention as I work my shoulder out of its main socket and into its alternative position. It can stay there comfortably for a bit.

"How did you know I was here?" I figure they found the doll, but no, there it still stands in its hiding place. If only it's not out of memory or anything. It does have its own IP address. Possibly it's still streaming. If anyone out there is watching the live feed on the VideoDollies website, maybe that will bring help.

The harridan smiles. "Your sister. She spilled her guts."

I stare at June. She doesn't even look like herself.

"When? I didn't hear her."

No response, just a sneer.

June didn't say anything. Plus I realize that if she did, it was the influence of the drugs. Or the ring. Or magic. But still, it hurts.

They dump out my pack on the foot of June's bed.

Sorting through that shiny magpie's nest, they hold up item after item, even my toothbrush and change of underwear. Apparently they're looking for something in particular.

Arlene stomps in, glaring right at me. "Where is it, you scheming twat?"

I blink innocently.

She snatches up my pack and shakes it upside-down. "I know it's in here. I can feel its presence. Must be a secret compartment. Aha!" She turns the pack inside out and rips the zippers open to empty every last corner and hidey-hole. Something heavy and hard tumbles out at June's feet.

The grimoire.

It didn't even try to hide. Closing my eyes momentarily, I prepare for it to tattle on me and go happily back to Arlene. But when she snatches it up, she blinks. (I had to peek.) Hoping against hope that it is pretending to be a math textbook, I hold my breath.

Arlene turns on me in anger. "Why do you have this—this ridiculous fable thing instead of my BOOK?!"

"What book?" I play innocent. Especially since I have no idea what it's pretending to be, anything from Shakespeare to the Blue Fairy Book. "I brought that so you could read it to us."

She snorts, not a pretty sight. "Don't give me that shit. Who carries around a stupid Gideon Bible? Two of them, in fact," she says, snatching up my grandmother's New Testament from the bed and shaking it mercilessly.

I wince, but suppress any smart remarks in hopes that she won't tear it to pieces.

"No, you're up to something." She tosses my grandmother's gift in the corner and turns the larger book back and forth in her hands. She runs her palms over the cover, probably noticing that it's no longer covered with that strange material, but with smooth boards. Her eyes glint. "Oh, I see. You've enchanted my book, have you? Well, I can unlock any spell done by an amateur. The book has a lock mode, and that's what I left it in."

She assumes the position. Not the one the cops put offenders in, but the sorceress position, kind of like a setter pointing at a felled duck. She bends her knees and extends her arms in front of her witchily, fingers like claws.

"All that cheerleading practice has really proven useful," I murmur.

Her eyes flash. "*Strazvet!*" booms out of her mouth. She whops the book with a short carved staff that I hadn't noticed hanging off her belt and shouts her magic word again. I can feel power exiting her like thunderbooms.

The tome won't budge from being a Bible.

After several more tries with various words of power (at least I assume that's what they are), Arlene is livid. She's as pale as I've ever seen her, and it makes her look ancient and weathered. Beating the book with the staff only makes it look beaten-up and weathered.

She finally heaves the book at me. "This really is a stupid Bible. This cretin carries it around, like maybe she's got religion." She barks out a laugh at the very idea. "Well, good luck with that." Turning to the acolytes, she tells them, "Search her things again. You're looking for a leatherbound tome about the size of that stupid thing."

I clutch the grimoire, hoping it has some help in store for me. Maybe it has turned against her because she is so wicked and it is good, or at least it is neutral and she has worn out her welcome. Or this might even mean it has had a change of heart and is now on my side. I can only hope.

I'll bet that over all these years of use and abuse, the book has never been thanked or even appreciated. Maybe not in hundreds or thousands of years. Impulsively (I seem to be all impulsive lately) I bear-hug it and whisper, "No matter how this comes out, I thank thee for all thy help. Thou hast tried, and I appreciate everything. It's all good."

"Stop that praying!" Arlene shrieks as she runs up in front of me. She shakes me by the shoulders so hard my teeth rattle. "Don't defy me. I will have what is mine."

She's triggering my fear of being beaten up. It has struck my usually agile tongue dumb.

Her hot breath blowing down my face, she snarls, "Be sure that I'll get the book back. You're only causing me a bit of extra hassle, because I'll have to waste a calling spell to Summon it back. We don't need to be distracted with searching for it when we need to finish our business with you ASAP."

"What business?" I managed to choke out, my voice not even sounding like my own (but rather like Pee-Wee Herman's, if his head were caught in a bear trap).

The lioness roars. "Where's my book?"

I goggle at her. Her veins really are pulsing blue at her temples.

She's nose-to-nose with me, and the smell of vetiver and patchouli on her is overwhelming. Not to mention garlic and onions on her breath from those pizzas. "That tome is my prize possession, do you understand? It's unbelievably arcane and powerful, and I have complete control over it. Someday, with its help, I will be dominant over those who have hindered me." Sounds ominous. "I want to know what you did with it. And pronto!"

"I hid it," I blurt on another impulse. "In the alley. So you couldn't get it back and make it do your evil deeds."

She laughs, a sound like fluorescent lights shattering in a parking garage. "Evil deeds! You're a stitch. Too bad you can't come over to our side, with that thirteen-year-old buzzsaw mind of yours. We could use some of those smarts. But I could never trust you, could I?"

"Why not?"

Her big eyes roll upward like two hard-boiled eggs with olive slices for irises. "Because." Whipping around to face the others again, she says, "Get out there and search the alley. Bring me anything you find that could be the book in disguise. And be quick about it."

You'd think the Keystone Cops had been dispersed, with nine of them bumbling off and trying to squeeze through the door at the same time, looking absolutely incompetent.

I hope there is a skunk or something worse living in that dumpster, and I hope it chews their ankles to shreds.

Arlene goes over and props June up, stuffing pillows
behind her back and head. June is a limp Raggedy Ann,
glassy-eyed, hanging from her hands cuffed to the headboard. My cousin sighs heavily.

"After we take what we want from April, then what?
What do I do with them?" Arlene mutters as if to herself.

One of the two remaining scruffballs shrugs. "They'll
just go into the trade. Won't they?"

"Not these two. Can't risk it." She erases the idea flatly.
"They're just smart enough to figure out some way to
escape and give it all away. This one"—indicating me
with a sweep of her right hand—"would run straight to
CNN. No, it's too chancy. They've got to be disposed of."

I feel hollow-chested. Like something ate part of my
intestines. This is my favorite cousin, the person I always
looked up to, whom I thought of as being something
special. I always believed our love for her was recipro-
cated. That her sometimes gruff manner with us was
"just her way." Because I knew she was a Stoic, in the
Greek sense of not showing much emotion except for a
reason, such as being a drama queen to get her way or to
scare people and get a rise out of them.

But…she didn't love us. At least she doesn't now. In
fact, she doesn't even see us as people. We're truffles she
can use to squeeze out the rich center, take something
that she's interested in right now, and then dump like
used tissues.

It turns out as I listen that by "join the trade" they
don't mean we could be taken on as apprentices to learn
the trade of sorcery, after all. They're talking about a

slave trade of sorts. Apparently they've taken young girls before, and when they've removed what they want, they funnel the girls into a network of sex or fetish slaves. I've heard of stuff like this in Thailand and other countries. But here? I'm seriously bummed that it can still go on right here in America.

So much for idealism.

For a while one of the two guys pleads our case, asking her to release us because "like, it's your cousins and all, so if you tell them not to get you in trouble they won't," and I almost feel a bit of gratitude towards him for it. Maybe he isn't beyond redemption like the others. He attempts to get her to let us go back home if we swear on the memory of John Lennon (or in June's case Kurt Cobain) never to say anything. He tells her he thinks we'll keep her secrets, and she knows we always have, so I think he might get somewhere. But ultimately he backs down.

"All right, I agree," says Tweedle-dumb finally. "They'd be problems if we kept them around, because they're rebellious."

Arlene is glowering. She snaps her fingers.

"We've got to convene. Consult the powers to guide us from here." She sends a glance full of contempt my way. "But first, I'm going to see what is taking them so long out there. They should've found the book by now." Buttonholing the yes-men, she tells them, "You two stay here and guard the door. Keep an eye on both of them. They're slicker than they look, so feel free to clobber them if they try anything. Hard." Looking Heavenward (and I don't know why, as she isn't cooperating with the angels), she announces, "Once I round everyone up, we'll go into my private domain. We have to confer on exactly how to dispose of them."

She swoops out like a vulture headed for a street kill.

It's really quiet in here. "Dispose" is not a word with lots of potential for getting away alive.

The two idiots glance at each of us. June is again unresponsive (apparently), and of course I'm tied up and they have no clue that I'm double-jointed and have been wiggling loose with that shoulder. In a bit they settle down, one on the stack of lumber and the other on another see-sawing chair near the door.

If these are her two top men—left-hand and right-hand—she definitely isn't recruiting from Mensa.

"May I read the Scriptures to myself?" I ask them. I put on my pitiful-child face and make my lip tremble. It's not tough to work up a couple of tears. "I need to pray."

They look at each other again. "Sure, girlie," says the one who was defending me for a while. "What can it hurt?" he says to the other one. "The boss left that book with her."

The book allows me to open it, which I take as a sign of encouragement. In fact, letters are already inking themselves on the page. I know the drill, so I read it aloud.

> *"Gently drift away*
> *From the cares of today,*

Take a quiet rest
It's all a funny jest
You two who watch it
Will now sleep and not botch it,
Whatever I do, you shall not scotch it.
Until your mistress should return,
Slumber gently and do not discern.
Sleep tight — Out goes the light!"

Our two guards zonk out, their heads lolling on their fat necks. "Bless you for a spell that knows when to work," I tell the grimoire, giving it a pat.

I look at June. She's still propped up. Her first words to me are, "You dummy. Why didn't you call the cops or go get help?"

She's right, of course.

"*Nos morituri te salutamus.*" Leave it to June to quote one of Gary's Latin phrases, which he uses to be dramatic whenever Lynwood serves something icky at dinner. It translates as, "We who are about to die salute you." Her voice is raspy. She seems dehydrated and she looks about to cry.

"June...."

"We've been wicked," she says. "If we die, I hope we go to Heaven. I've been lying here repenting. You need to do the same." She's silently crying.

I've never heard my sister admit to any belief system other than "whoever dies with the most toys wins."

For some reason—for obvious reasons, I suppose—over the past few days I have had in the back of my mind the idea of Heaven and how I should be looking to it rather than to the book and the hidden powers. At night I've dreamed of a distant parade of people and animals (most especially dogs and cats, but with lions and lambs in the lead, all garlanded about their necks with pale flowers). The people are those who were lost but are now recovered, reunited at last, wearing soft tangerine robes and holding hands. Everyone's singing (even the dogs, especially the dogs) and they sound so sweet and in harmony with each other that you know from the song that no one is alone or searching for anything. No one is wanting or striving. Yet they're moving like the elegant runners I have seen who seem to make their flight over the earth so effortlessly and whose strides fall in unison somehow, unconsciously, I think. The procession is long. In fact, it has no end. The parade is infinite.

I wish that in the distance I could be assured that all of the lost people—the innocent, the confused, the hated (and the animals too, who are said to be "dumb" in so many ways and supposedly never know their place in the world, yet still seem to know love—and what else is there, really)—I wished that they were finally there and that they could sing at last and that the lion would lead us like Aslan in those Narnia books I used to love so much until Gary took them away because he heard on the Rationalists' Network that they were some kind of religious analogy or parable or some such, but in my dream the lion and lamb not only could lie down together but were leading us in the right way, toward the Ultimate Source, the Light that everyone dying tends to speak of in their last moments, as they're leaving us to go forward into whatever is our ultimate destiny.

But it seems more and more each day that the truth recedes from us: life grows dark and everything we've known is snuffed out in a gasp of fear. Our spirits fly to the unknown, leaving nothing behind but flesh to rot and memories to plague the living.

"Dear Universe, I'm sorry about everything, especially the fooling around with black magic and so forth," I say, trying to pray, but something is blocking my prayer. So much for repenting, at least right now.

June is babbling now. "We'll go to Grandma. Go towards the light, April, and you'll see her. Look, I see her. And Grandpa. And Mischief!" Our fat old cat. "They're waiting for us. They're smiling and nodding. Their arms are wide open. We're coming! Wait; I've got to get April and bring her with me." She smiles. "I love you, world. Thank you, Universe, that You allowed us to be some of the mud that got to sit up and look around. O Heaven, paradise forever, we're coming."

June has gone bye-bye. It is up to me to figure out how to escape.

Where is my head? It's time to break loose.

I pop my shoulder back into the first position and then move it back and forth, loosening the ropes little by little. Wiggling like a snake works pretty well because these people don't even know how to tie someone up properly. Especially a double-jointed someone.

Slowly the ropes slide and slip and finally give, and I get my right arm free. I use my right hand to loosen the ropes holding my left arm and hand. Scooting the chair just a bit allows me to reach the shards of my smartphone. But will it power on?

The screen is cracked and the frame is broken, but perhaps I can get it to make one last call. I press the wake-up button and suck in a breath.

The button falls off, pinging gently on the floor between my toes. I can see the green circuit board underneath, which is broken in fourths like a graham cracker.

The book vibrates softly in my lap. "I haven't forgotten you," I reassure it, patting it. "You have been my guide and have mostly helped me, even though you had to show those awful pictures that weren't true. That wasn't your fault. I forgive you for that and all's even between us. I do wish you could help me now."

Wait! This is a magical grimoire. If I can read spells out of it, why can't I write spells in it?

If it's willing, and it seems to be, as it lets me open its covers to (of course) a blank page.

Coaxing out of my side pocket the purple-ink gel pen I always carry, I briefly apologize to the pages I'm about to deface. My drawing is right around stick-figure level.

On the first page I write *HELP! EMERGENCY!* And then I sketch June and myself tied up, hanging over a cauldron full of fire (that should grab attention). I caption it, "Fire at Cosmodemonic Telecom warehouse in East St. Louis, Missouri, where we are being held by psychos. Send help." As an afterthought I add, "Don't use sirens."

The book needs to send this by snailmail, fax, e-mail (although I have already sent out e-mail, but did that even reach its destination?), or the ectoplasmic interstitial hoodoo express, I don't care which, as long as the picture appears instantly on everyone's screen or in the magazine they're reading or via the junk mail they're currently tearing open (whatever works). A great ancient-magic tome should be able to handle that if a palm-sized hunk of plastic can transmit information wirelessly across the miles, right? I don't know how to tell it to proceed, so I have to go on a wing and a prayer.

In a TO: box I list everyone who should get this: first Lynwood, Gary, and Justin Fink (it might be the last communication he ever sees from me, so I draw a heart and "XOX" next to his name.) The picture needs to go to the local police and fire departments (thus the fire in the cauldron—no fire company will be able to resist that), so I write, "Police and fire agencies of St. Louis." As an afterthought, I write in all the e-mail addresses I can remember from our homeschool group. As the woman who tinkled in the ocean said, "It couldn't hurt."

Then I say aloud, "Send the picture however you can. By mail, by snail, or over whichever Information Superhighway you can, flash priority. Make it appear before their very eyes. Hurry, please. I know you can do it." How lame of me to encourage it as if it's a trained seal, but whatever it takes to communicate. "Thank you, O Powers."

The book seems to understand. The sketches slowly fade like disappearing ink.

I cradle the book on my lap for a moment more. Then I turn to a new page and sketch that ring sliding off of June's finger. No wonder artists complain that hands are tough to draw.

"June," I whisper, "can you get the ring off?"

She's silent. "Stuck," she says in a frog-voice.

Sighing, I give the book a consoling rub across the paper. "At least we tried. Endora couldn't take off Samantha's spells, after all." The paper warms under my touch. "Even if you can't send the messages"—because I don't know for certain whether that worked or was beyond its abilities—"I really appreciate everything you have been able to do. You did good."

I give the book a tight hug to thank it again. Then it starts to wiggle. I don't know at first what it's got in mind, but then I get the strong feeling that I'd better drop it. Against my heart, I allow myself one last squeeze and let it fall to the concrete floor.

I tell June, who is still sitting there staring into space, "We've got to get out of this room *now*. Can you walk?"

My sister shakes her head and bursts into tears again.

The door crashes open, squealing almost off its hinges. I grab my ropes just as Arlene and the crew burst back in, fuming.

I panic because she's surely going to notice that the two dummies are even dumber now...but somehow the spell knows when to quit, and the guards startle briefly and come to, blinking. They glance at each other, and a silent agreement passes between them. Probably that they should say nothing at all, since after all "nothing happened" while they were out.

"Little liar," Arlene addresses me. Her face is wreathed in frowns, wrapped in a livid mask of hatred. Then she notices that I'm untied. She whirls furiously on the guards, who jump to their feet. "Why are you just sitting there when she's getting loose? What's wrong with you?"

"I don't know," Tweedle-dumb begins, but falls silent as Arlene whirls back to me and re-ties my bonds, this time tying my chest and neck to the chair as tightly as she probably dares. Her minions clog the doorway behind her.

"It's time to be done with you," she declares.

"You're going to kill us," I say to Arlene. It's not so much a question as a realization. No, an admission to myself. I've been in denial about this, at least a little.

"Of course I am." She steps forward and seizes the grimoire. "There was no book, nothing useful out there, not even in the dumpster." Her gaze lasers me. "It suddenly occurred to me that you'd find some clever way to screw this thing up. That's why I didn't know right away for sure that this is it."

She attempts to brandish it at me, but the book is like a lump of clay as she handles it, or maybe more like a limp magazine that's been drowned in the bathtub. It flops back and forth in her hands as she tries to open it. She looks as if she'd like to tear it in half the way those stuntmen used to do with thick phone books, but whatever she does to it just deforms it and doesn't seem to damage it. It still doesn't want to open for her.

"The magical lock must be malfunctioning. I'll need a potion, probably," she mutters. Then she addresses the book sternly. "I'll deal with you later. I don't need you for this, anyway." She tosses it carelessly at June's feet.

She should've been a middle manager. She has all the skills.

I look at Arlene's opaque eyes and the ruthless set of her pointed chin and realize that in the past when I've gazed at her in wonder and admiration, I've been seeing a "loving cousin" illusion of my own making. Maybe for years. I don't know this person at all.

"So why us?" I ask her as she eyes me appraisingly. "There are lots of people out there."

"You were dumb enough to come." She smiles.

"But…." She's got me there. "We only started out because your boyfriend was looking for you and we thought you were in trouble."

"Ah, Diderich." She sighed into the distance. "He always misunderstood. He thought my having sex with him implied that I wanted anything else to do with him."

"You sent him. Along with the messages we got through the book."

"I knew you were the smart one."

The Hoodie Guy (Diderich, is it, now. At last I have a name) is standing in the doorway looking perturbed. Hope he didn't catch that, or else he might be surprised at hearing for the first time how insignificant he is.

"I still don't understand. Why prey on your two favorite cousins?"

"Why you? Why anybody?" She seems consumed with her own thoughts. "You always thought you were better than me. Well, you're not. But you're finally good for something, at last."

Wow. I never knew she felt that way. It would have been healthier for her to express this years ago instead of letting her feelings fester to this point.

June croaks out, "But I was your favorite, your special pet. I came to save you."

Arlene shrugs. "Nothing's done for altruistic reasons. We do what we do for reasons of self-interest. Haven't you read Ayn Rand, if you're so smart? You should have watched out for your own self-interest."

The ultimate blow is that she double-crossed us. No, the ultimate blow is that she did that, and she just… doesn't…care.

Not anymore, anyway.

June rallies one last time. "But you're in so much trouble. They're already trying to put you in boot camp. If you hurt us, you'll get in even more trouble."

Arlene takes on a faraway look. "Speaker Bensh says, 'We all want to avoid trouble, but that's where the treasure is.'"

Whoever that freak is, that's not even philosophy, just a tagline. Arlene has frankly gone on the ride to Nowheresville. And she plans to push us down the hill in front of her. All the way.

"All right. We're over; I can accept that." I can't help the whiny tone in my voice. "But why can't you just let us go?"

"The Powers have given their consent. We will use your deaths to gain far greater power." She tilts her head. "But not before I get what I came after in the first place. Let's get this over with."

The two scruffy guards have no problem extracting me from the chair and preparing me despite my struggle. As I'd expected, they rub a gel all over my arms and legs and chest, something that takes away my energy and will. A witches' ointment like the ones back in old Salem, I'm sure. Too bad this one's not for flying like those were.

I drift into a kind of twilight sleep as they lay me out on the floor and I go under the sheet.

They're going to take my math talent.

playing with fire

When I wake up, it stinks of patchouli and everything looks tinged with blue. As if I've been out in the sun too long and my vision is color-shifted. I close my eyes again and reopen them, but I'm still awake.

I try to add two and two, but my mind doesn't contain the concept of "addition." I can't remember how to add or subtract. The idea of "subtract" fades even as I try to retrieve it. What could it mean? Mathematical operations of all kinds are gone.

In fact, I don't think I could count to ten. Absolutely not past ten. What's the word for ten plus one? It begins with "A," I'm almost sure, but it slips away into the ether and is lost to me, laughing as it escapes forever.

I keep blinking. My brain feels different. What comes to mind is an old proverb I read somewhere: We must shed everything, our old skin, pride, and ego included, before we are transformed. This relates back to the thoughts about going to Heaven, also a major transformation.

The black-clad group stands ready to form their circle on command. They release June's hands from the cuffs (possibly because the metal would interfere with their spell; I read that somewhere, probably in Tolkien), and she winces as the feeling apparently starts to return to her fingers. I know she must still be weak, because I certainly am. They squash me next to June on the cot, and we're both bound to the mattress by ropes around our waists and ankles. We're just so much firewood to them.

I suppose I'd better finish up that repenting.

Arlene smiles, assuming her cheerleader persona. "Now that we have extracted everything useful from these two, let's thank the Powers in the special way."

With a sacrifice to feed their personal demons and increase their power.

All I can think of is the plot of the Beatles' film "Help!" and how the bad guys were chasing Ringo to sacrifice him…and the Indiana Jones flick where the Thuggee cult magicked the heart out of a guy…and June's beloved war movies, because war of any kind is a form of human sacrifice. No, really all I can think of is how I hate pain and I don't want this to hurt. That's all I can ask, I guess.

The ritual to kill us begins.

In Arlene's hands I notice a silver blade engraved with runes. Easily, as if it were a trophy for her old roller derby team, Arlene pushes it overhead between clasped hands and begins to chant, shuddering with power.

She becomes suffused with a glow of black light. That's the only name I can call it. It's not the UV light you can get at joke gift stores, from purple bulbs, but actually black. Although you wouldn't think light could be black. Trust me, this was.

She nods to the scruffiest of her acolytes. He breaks out of the circle as everyone drops hands. He strides around the perimeter of the room, raising his arms to shoulder level. As he makes the square, he dips to one side and then the other, like a light plane waving its wings to people on the ground. His fingers work and wiggle as if he's playing a keyboard. All the while, he hums a minor scale. Sounds like E minor.

It's pretty creepy.

Quivering all over, he comes to a stop in front of me. Both his hands land gently on my face. He puts his thumbs on my forehead, his fingertips on cheeks and chin. They burn like ice cubes. When he removes them, I realize he has swiped some kind of makeup or paint on me. Traditional markings, probably. For the kill.

He falls to his knees and keens out, "Offered to Oryanwen."

In a minute he rises and makes his way over to June. A glance at Arlene confirms she's watching all this with relish, as are the others who formed the circle earlier. He does the same with June. I see her marks are orange and black. That good old Halloween theme. On his knees, he shouts, "Offered to Asmodeus."

Now Arlene steps forward. Her eyes glitter. "O Powers, accept these sacrifices as our payment for increased prowess in your service," she sings tunelessly. I think it's in the same key the other guy was in. She looks like the high priestess of Bast out of a book I have about ancient Egypt. This is SO not the Arlene I remember. But then I knew that already.

She swings her hands down, still clasped in a prayerlike position, until they point out in front of her. Between her palms I see the flash of her blade. She continues her chant in the ancient rhythm, but I can't understand her words. Maybe it's the true incantatory poetry.

I steel myself against being skewered. Or having the life sucked out of me into the blade. Or just disappearing in a flash of green light. I close my eyes and wait.

When nothing happens for several beats, I open my eyes. Arlene's expression is beyond perplexed. She repeats the last few words, then stares at me as if I'm simply not cooperating.

I glance around the circle and see the others staring down at the foot of the bed. They're looking at...the grimoire.

The book's glowing that same sort of freaky blue-black light that suffuses Arlene. It's not hot or cold, because neither my feet nor June's flinch away.

As the book grows brighter and brighter, its covers flip open and its pages flutter. It shudders and starts making an eerie noise like a ghost screaming. Yet metallic, like the theremin in *Forbidden Planet*. The acolytes back away, all the way against the walls, and a couple of them flee the room, evidently knowing better than to stand around while a thousand-year-old entity shaped like a book decides it's sick of playing Arlene's wicked games. The eerie noise is a B-flat, I think. The keening crescendos and then stops.

I hear a clang, like something hitting the steel footboard of the bed. June's ring clatters to the floor at our feet. Everyone stares at it in curiosity and confusion.

Freed of the ring's grip, June sits up straighter, pushing the pillows aside. Before anyone knows she's going to move again, her right hook shoots out and clocks Arlene on the end of her pointy nose. If her torso and feet weren't still bound to the mattress, I think she'd leap on our cousin the way that kid in *A Christmas Story* jumped the bully.

Arlene gasps as a gush of blood rushes out of her nostrils, and she falls against Tweedle-dumb, temporarily out of commission.

She deserves it.

June slumps back from the effort, and for some reason no one tries to restrain us.

Because everyone's gazes are again riveted to the grimoire. It's glowing more and more strongly. I hear the tuneless tune in my head again. The book begins to throw off sparks like an Independence Day sparkler.

There's a bright flash, and the book turns to ash.

I stare at the ashes as they glow blue, then purple, then wink out altogether.

There's nothing left. I burst into tears.

A white dove emerges from the ashes. She circles once or twice around my head and then escapes through the broken window to freedom in the sky. I am not sure if I really saw this or just imagined it. Either way, it was real.

Arlene has mashed one of her sleeves up against her bloody nose. (June can pack quite a punch.) Tweedle supports her from the back as she waves her other arm over her head. Weakly, she chants an incantation. There's a tiny puff of smoke, as if she had blown one of her famous smoke rings, and then…nothing.

Out of the corner of my eye there's a flashing light. Am I imagining it? Is it THE light? Should I go toward it? But it's alternating between red and blue, not a steady white as you'd expect from the angels.

Evidently someone took the "silent approach" suggestion in my messages seriously. Those flashing lights are on the street below. There's a crash, and I twist to see the hook-and-ladder engine extending its long ladder up to our window. Meanwhile, the fire company pounds up the fire escape dragging a muslin hose.

"Where's the fire?" asks a burly bearded fireman.

"I might ask the same of *you*," huffs Arlene. Her knife and her aura of blackness are gone. She's just another Goth teen hanging with her homies.

"Help?" I say weakly. I thought that I would be much louder, but my personal energy is almost entirely drained.

He glances my way. *Two girls on the bed together?* His dirty thoughts are fairly transparent.

Then he apparently notices we are tied up.

Two cops enter stage right, from the doorway everyone has been using. Evidently, there's another way upstairs that's easier than my route.

The first officer starts sawing away at my ropes, and
others minister to June. She's moaning and I realize she
might be worse off physically than I had realized. In fact,
EMS is coming in the doorway with oxygen and a rolling stretcher.

Arlene pastes on her regretful look and tries to explain herself, feebly. "This might look kind of strange,"
she begins.

The first cop just smiles gruffly and says, "Sorry, honey,
we saw the video on the way over." Another cop glow-
ers at Arlene.

"It was just a little prank," Tweedle insists to a female
officer holding an important-looking clipboard. "Initiation into our gang—I mean, our crew. You know." He
plucks at the shoulder of his black tee. I suppose he's
going to claim their gang colors are black and black.

"Uh-huh," the cop says in a neutral tone. "Hilarious,
isn't it." She jingles her handcuffs.

Arlene looks like she swallowed a Gila monster.

chapter the end

We have been rescued.

We're outside, on the sidewalk, next to the EMS engine. June has an oxygen mask over her nose and mouth, which worries me, but at least she's sitting up. I'm on another of the rolling stretchers being checked out by the firemen. They want to know where I got all the bruises that are now breaking out from my fall earlier. I have no problem letting them think they resulted from the efforts of Arlene's bad crowd.

"Thank you for coming," I say, Lynwood's Southern manners not deserting me.

"We couldn't do anything else," said the guy who keeps taking my blood pressure, alternating between my upper arms. "First the dispatcher received an odd phone call that got cut off abruptly, but it reported a fire here. Then we got this weird fax and a bunch of phone calls coming in from clear across the country demanding that we go check this place out immediately. Some hysterical woman called from Texas claiming her daughters are being held captive. Last straw was, some kid sent us a video link to some wild antics. Glad we came."

I'm still not sorry that we were dumb enough to come to rescue our cousin. That was the right and proper thing to do. Would I do it again, if I were forewarned and could handle all of this differently?

I can't answer that.

A police officer dials home for us and hands me his cell phone. I tell Lynwood, "We thought Arlene was in trouble."

Gary's on the extension. "So you went running out there and expected to fly in like the Powerpuff Patrol to rescue her."

How does he know about the Powerpuffs?

Lynwood's voice on the phone is barely controlled. Any moment she could become hysterical. "I'm not going to scold you girls now," she begins. "I'm too relieved. You're runaways, so the authorities are bringing you home immediately on a Southwest flight. We'll meet you at Love Field." After she gasps noisily for air (this indicates she could start sobbing anytime), she adds, "And unblock your cell phones, or whatever you've done. I filled your voicemail the first night you were gone."

"We'll be talking about all this later," says Gary in a tone that I know is supposed to be ominous, but there's too much joy in his voice at having found us alive and pretty much unharmed for me to be upset.

A police escort sounds so official, and plenty safe. I sleep in the ambulance and doze off in a chair at the police station and snore on the airplane home. June is a little more alert, and I wake on the flight to find she's sitting next to me holding my hand. When she realizes I'm awake, she doesn't drop it immediately the way she normally would. She gives it a squeeze before releasing it.

Coming off the plane at Love, our police escort makes people think we're in custody (which we are) because we're under arrest (which we're not). I kind of enjoy that. June walks with her head held high, dismissing the idea of what anyone else thinks.

Oddly enough, Justin meets us at the gate of the Southwest terminal. He's talking too fast, like he's got to get it out before he forgets.

"Your rescue was live on CNN," he babbles. I can hardly understand him as his words tumble out. "I sent video clips to their I-Witness user site and somebody there was awake. You were live on Dallas Channel Eight, too, for part of the time; they have the ability to pick up a live feed like the one VideoDollies runs." Who knew? "They have the video of that thing they did to your sister on their website."

"Wow," I say as he wraps me in a very brief hug.

"Yeah," he says, releasing me as if he doesn't realize the Great Import of my First Hug From A Guy Who Is Not A Relative. "First I called the cops up there and told them, "Witches have my next-door girlfriend and her sister,' but I don't think they believed me. Still, I kept blathering, and they transferred me to some woman sergeant. I said that you'd been kidnapped by a cult your cousin was in, a group that was about to do a human sacrifice, and they'd better get over there before history repeated itself. And that I was about to call the press. Which is the next thing I did. I phoned the Post-Dispatch using their contact number off the Web. The reporter seemed kind of confused. Did he come out there?" He's waving come-hither to someone back in the terminal.

"I don't know. There might have been some flash-bulbs going off once we got outside. But you did right. I know it helped."

GIRLFRIEND echoes in my ears. Of course he was just exaggerating for the cops. He means, I'm a girl, I'm his friend. But still.

"Your parents are here. They let me drive them."

And now come running Lynwood and Gary. That was who he was motioning to. He must've asked for a moment alone. I can't believe Lynwood gave it to him, but maybe she was composing herself.

She lifts me off my feet into a full embrace. Gary snatches me up and we twirl twice. June gets the same treatment. Then we have a group hug. We'll be heading to the car in a huddle, like the cast of a television show leaving the set for the last time.

It's hotter here in Texas. I peel off my hoodie and find I'm sweaty.

"I'm so glad they didn't do anything to you." Lyn-wood kisses the top of my head.

"That could be seen as a misstatement," June mum-bles. Her lips and cheeks are bruised and I don't know whether to comment on it; it could've been done by the EMS team's efforts, or it could've been from being slapped in the ritual. "They didn't leave us completely untouched."

"Oh, I see that, sweetie." Lynwood envelops her again. "Lips heal fastest, though. You'll be fine right away. I meant they didn't take—anything important."

"Only our innocence," she says in a sarcastic tone. Everyone looks totally gobsmacked, and then she laughs. "Not like that, people. Get your minds out of the gutter."

That's when I know she's going to be okay.

And so am I.

As they say in the movies, I learned something. Maybe it wasn't stuff I wanted to know, but apparently the Universe thought I needed to. We had an exciting adventure. I will get my pack and most of my stuff back eventually, courtesy of the police, so I didn't lose anything irreplaceable.

The math, right. I don't miss it as much as you'd think. It's seeping back, maybe: I can count past ten again. Not being able to felt weird. And I think I dreamed about long division when I dozed off on the plane.

Wouldn't it be a kick if all those people they sold talents to lost them after a short time? Maybe they just took the electrical activity or something out of that part of the brain and sold that. The original traces and neurons or whatnot, they're all still there in my brain. So it might be that our talents will slowly grow back, and those buyers will end up mightily peeved when theirs don't last.

Not my problem. I learned why you don't rollerskate in the derby unless you're a pro. In other words, Arlene got in over her head. She was just too confident to know any better.

I don't know what'll happen to her, if anything. I can't worry about it right now. I've got enough to handle with myself and June and Lynwood and Gary and college coming up in a few years. Maybe not that many; they're talking about starting us at a community college that has a high school/college credit early start program. June and I could go together. We could stay out of trouble that way, if we were busier and more focused. That's the drift of their thinking, anyway. I wouldn't mind. I like school.

June has closed herself up in her room to read teen magazines.

Even minus (ha) the effects of the ring, she's still growing away from me. She teases her hair now and has a couple of plastic tiaras for when she feels "girly." Teen reality television is beginning to interest her. She actually wears the makeup Lynwood buys.

We're too sophisticated for the treehouse. Those days are gone forever, I guess. I knew the time would come. Just not this soon.

We are famous, by the way. Actually, we're having our fifteen minutes of fame. June's video went viral and some of the other footage has shown up, edited and unedited, on all manner of sites. Some are mocking, some claim it is a warning to careless youth, but all of them show our faces, even if it's in shadow and lighted mostly by flickering candle-flame. It'll blow over. That stuff always does. But it'll be archived. The 'net is forever. So if anyone anytime wants to know about it, whoop, there it is.

All I'm going to say about it, though, is it's a freakin' lucky break that we don't go to school. I can only imagine the kind of razzing and teasing and shunning normal kids would pull on us. And it would probably never stop. We're still recognized sometimes, a couple of weeks out. I may change my name to Tallulah and let Lynwood bleach me blonde.

Justin and I are friends. We don't have to watch him through the spyglass any more. June has a new friend online who might be a guy and who might be coming to meet her someday. They're gaming together almost every evening on a multi-player site. Her avatar is a platypus with wings. She seems no worse for wear, although she does trip over things and bangs the doors and drawers more than she ever did.

I'm still sad about the grimoire. It had a good heart. I miss having someone—I mean, something, or *whatever*—that seemed to care about me and could anticipate what I needed to do before I even knew it. Maybe someday I'll find a person who is like that.

Here's hoping the grimoire has discharged whatever curse was on it to make it be a book of evil for a time, and now it has gone to wherever good books go. The great library in the sky, I suppose.

Or maybe the book didn't commit hari-kiri but only sent itself somewhere else, and I'll run across it again during my earthly journey. Who can say?

I don't know what happened to June's ring. I didn't see anyone pick it up. It might still be on the floor in the abandoned warehouse. But somebody will eventually get hold of it, and we can only hope that when the book negated Arlene's spells, it negated *all* of them....

Have I mentioned I hate change? Even though most of the recent change has been for the better, I'm still in a period of adjustment.

You might tell me to get over it and "man up." That I should simply accept that some things come to an end, like the book and our friendship with Arlene. Well, I can't help asking. Is belief enough? Or is there more out there than we know? As Shakespeare once wrote, "There are more things in Heaven and Earth than are dreamt of in your philosophy."

I've come to realize that in this world, thought and reason are often replaced with knee-jerk emotional reactions, pseudo-religions such as the worship of the Almighty Dollar, or out-of-control materialism that puts us completely out of touch with the things that are really important.

But I suspect the wholesale rejection of religion and the spiritual realm is a bad mistake. Whether or not we want to acknowledge the unseen and respect it, let alone come under its authority, it is still there and must be examined. Just like in the thirteenth century, when the earth revolved around the sun whether or not anyone believed it. Truth does exist. Should we not seek it?

Maybe it sounds as if I'm saying you must see life in a new way or be awakened to The Great Mystery. Well...I suppose maybe I am.

We must examine ourselves so that even if we don't embrace any organized religion, we won't miss the greater journey. I believe we were put here for a reason. We need to learn how to stop focusing only on our own needs and start helping each other. There is nothing else. Power, material gains, lording it over someone...that all counts for nothing in the greater scheme.

As Jimi Hendrix once said, when the power of love overcomes the love of power, the world will know peace.

Lynwood and Gary don't spend quite as much time working these days. They stay home with us sometimes and do nothing at all. We have mandatory mealtimes together, even if they're working and have important projects, where we all eat the same thing and everyone gets to speak what's on his or her mind. I think they're really enjoying it. "There's no place like home" might be a cliché, and so is "despite rough currents, we abide and we endure." But clichés survive because there's a large grain of truth in them.

Why am I not all bitter and hardened? Why don't I have psychotic symptoms and why am I not confined to the treehouse with PTSD? I've even stopped biting my cuticles, and my nails are starting to get long. It's a paradox and a puzzle. Just lucky, I guess.

June sometimes accuses me of being unreasonably optimistic, and I suppose that's fair enough. Optimism seems increasingly out of place in this world, but whether that alone is sufficient reason to abandon it I'm still not sure.

All I know is that we have today, and we'd better seize it. None of us has extra time to waste in sulking or flailing. We could be snatched through the Veil anytime, by some trick of fate, some unexpected destiny. There's still so much that I want to see and know, and the important thing is to do what I was put here on Earth to do. After I figure it out, of course.

Everyone has to figure that out for themselves.

Figure what out, you might ask? I mean: Find your mission in life. I believe everyone has one, and lots of people never find out what theirs is.

I bet that's something I'll never need to worry about.

about the author

Shalanna Collins is the pen name of an ex-hippie who's still wearing embroidered blue jeans, drop earrings, long Alice-in-Wonderland hair, and sandals. Also see her books written as Denise Weeks. *April, Maybe June* is the first in her series of The Bliss Sisters Magical Adventures.

Shalanna, maybe Denise, graduated from Southern Methodist University with a BS in Computer Science and a BA in Mathematics. When she isn't writing fiction, she tutors secondary school math, works as a literacy volunteer, does research on the Internet, and noodles on the piano.

Like many Texans, she doesn't intend to be funny, but often puts her own twisted spin on whatever she observes. Novelist, pianist, belly dancer, baton twirler (but no fire batons ever again, by order of the Renner, Texas, Fire Dep't), Shalanna has published fiction in several genres, including mystery, fantasy, chick lit, and romantic suspense.

Find her online:

shalanna.livejournal.com
shalannacollins.blogspot.com
deniseweeks.blogspot.com